Peter T has written six
much p *es from a Long*
Room. n. His credits
include *n't Know You*
Cared a es upon which
this boo

By the same author

A Touch of Daniel
Mog
I Didn't Know You Cared
Except You're a Bird
Stirk of Stirk
Shemerelda
Tales from a Long Room
More Tales from a Long Room

PETER TINNISWOOD

The Home Front

GRANADA

London Toronto Sydney New York

Published by Granada Publishing Limited in 1982

ISBN 0 586 05707 2

A Granada Paperback Original

Granada Publishing Limited
Frogmore, St Albans, Herts AL2 2NF
and
36 Golden Square, London W1R 4AH
866 United Nations Plaza, New York, NY 10017, USA
117 York Street, Sydney, NSW 2000, Australia
100 Skyway Avenue, Rexdale, Ontario, M9W 3A6, Canada
61 Beach Road, Auckland, New Zealand

Made and printed in Great Britain by
Cox and Wyman Ltd, Reading
Set in Times

Chapter One

I am a nosey sort of person.

In fact, I am extremely nosey.

I make no bones about it.

Why should I?

My name is Mrs Place.

I think in short paragraphs.

I talk in short paragraphs.

If more people did the same, the world would be a much better place.

Am I right?

I am.

Incidentally, what about that Oliver Newton-John?

Have you ever in the whole of your life heard a voice like it?

I haven't, and I spent most of the war years stuck with my mother in the Anderson shelter.

If only she'd married Cliff Richards, when she had the chance all those years ago and settled down to having babies and hoovering her pelmets and being argumentative, she'd have had no time to inflict her so-called singing on us.

It makes me sick.

It's the same with that woman in the dog biscuit shop.

She's never been the same with me since she had her ears syringed last Whitsuntide.

Since she's had no excuse for ignoring her husband's wittering, she's turned into a positive tartar.

There's just no pleasure in buying millet sprays from her these days.

Mind you, millet sprays have gone to the dogs, haven't they?

I remember the days when they lasted Cocky a full week.

All he gets out of a spray now is a breakfast and half his elevenses.

Cocky's my budgerigar in case you're wondering.

I think budgies make marvellous pets, don't you?

They're company.

Am I right?

I am.

And I'll tell you another thing – they're very clean about their person.

Meticulous.

I think they put some humans to shame the way they can scratch their ears standing on one leg.

Now then, being as how this book is all about me and my family, you'll want to know something about me and my background.

I don't blame you.

What's wrong with being nosey?

I am.

I was born into what I call a 'good' family.

All through the summer father wore a panama hat and an alpaca jacket. And in the winter he wore navy blue.

He was in textiles.

He had very small hands, had father, and he was meticulous with his fingernails.

He kept them in perfect nick.

His feet were on the small side, too.

He wore dove grey spats for business.

Every summer he took us for two weeks holiday to the Lake District in the Humber.

I loved the smell of its leather.

That's what's wrong with modern cars these days – they don't smell nice, do they?

And they look grumpy and discontented from the front.

Father's Humber was navy blue with bottle green piping, and it always seemed so content and at ease with the world.

When you opened the door to get in, it smiled at you, and it sang softly to itself as it bowled along the open road.

We lived in a comfortable house in the Halifax Road.

It was what I call a 'good' house.

It was built of stone, and it had a conservatory at the back, where father grew orchids and kept a tortoise called William.

Downstairs we had a drawing room with a turkey red carpet and a grandfather clock, a dining room with parquet flooring, a large kitchen with a black-lead range, a utility room where the maid did the washing in a large tub, a good-sized cloakroom and a study, where father did his accounts and smoked his pipe.

I loved the smell of father's pipe.

Upstairs we had four bedrooms and the usual offices.

There was a lovely garden at the back.

I liked it, anyway.

Mr Topper with the cork leg used to come in three times a week to help with the hard work.

Father tended to the flowers and the shrubs, and I fed the goldfish in the pond.

They're very interesting for fish, are goldfish.

A robin used to nest every year in an old kettle in the potting shed, and we had house martins in the eaves, too.

Father was very fond of cricket.

As for mother – well, she was an extremely nosey person like me.

It was Christmas week, and Mrs Place was preparing to visit her son, Hallam, in London.

Hallam was a writer of comedy scripts for television, and he lived in Wimbledon.

Mrs Place lived in a city in the north of England.

The winter was bleak.

Redwing and fieldfare starved in chapped-white fields. Canals creaked with ice. Frost-scorched ceanothus wilted in suburban gardens. Rooks hunched into arctic gales. Snow-drifted moorland hamlets cowered beneath leaded skies.

The price of sprouts was outrageous.

In her spotless lounge/diner Mrs Place handed over Cocky to the safe-keeping of her younger son, Garfield, and his wife, Hazel.

'Now think on, won't you?' she said. 'You've not to flap your arms in front of him suddenly, and you mustn't let him out of the cage if there's any of those nature programmes on the television. Well, all he does you see, Hazel, is stand in front of the telly pecking at David Attenborough, and I think that sort of thing could give him complexes later on in life, don't you, Garfield?'

'Yes,' said Garfield.

'Now then, you're to give him a millet spray every other day, and, if his motions should be loose, you've to give him two eyedropfuls of his medicine three times daily and take his cuttlefish bone off him. Do you follow me, Hazel?'

'Yes,' said Hazel.

It began to snow.

The flakes were damp and soft.

That's the trouble with pets – they're so tying when you want to go away, aren't they?

When I was little and we went away for two weeks each year to the Lake District, Mr Topper with the cork leg used to look after the Airedales.

I think they quite enjoyed it.

The maid looked after the tortoise, William, and the hyacinth macaw, and the golden-fronted fruitsucker and the two Manx cats.

When I was little, we always had a houseful of pets.

I think it's important for children to learn the value of pets.

That's why I always made sure Hallam and Garfield and their sister, Avril, were always surrounded by animals even though they did tend to pong a bit at the height of summer.

You see, if you keep goldfish in a bowl in the house, you must make sure you change their water regular.

It's the same with dogs – give them a dry shampoo three times a week, pop a Bob Martin's into their food on Friday nights, and you'll never be troubled by unsightly smells.

Am I right?

I am.

Next morning Mrs Place set off from her house for the station to catch the train to visit her son, Hallam, in London.

'I'm going to London to visit my son,' she said to the taxi driver.

'Pardon?' said the taxi driver.

'I'm going to London to visit my son. He's a script writer for the telly. His name's Hallam Place. He's very famous. Have you heard of him?'

'No,' said the taxi driver.

'All right. Please yourself,' said Mrs Place.

She settled herself into the back of the taxi cab.

It was a black Ford Granada with a white roof.

'Course what I regret most is the passing of the trams,' said Mrs Place.

'Do you?' said the taxi driver.

'Yes I do. I know they were somewhat of a traffic hazard, but, by heck, they did know how to shift the crowds.

'Am I right?

'I am.'

The taxi driver hunched his head into his simulated fur collar and switched up the radio.

Mrs Place popped a sulphur tablet into her mouth, eased a strap of her vest and looked out of the windows of the cab.

The black roofs of the houses in the valley below made diamonds in the snow.

Steam from the waste pipes of the mills coiled above the sluggish river. Globs of detergent slowly twirled on the surface of the yellowing waters. Sirens hooted. A barge lowed mournfully at the lockkeeper's hut.

Black smuts pocked the new-fallen snow.

I know what people think about the North.

They think it's all muck and living over the brush with women like Elsie Tanner.

Well, it isn't.

There's a part of the North that Southerners know nothing about.

Absolutely nothing.

I'm talking about the respectable North.

When I was little we always had satsumas at Christmas.

Without fail.

We had a box at the Theatre Royal for the Panto.

We had a sideboard full of mixed nuts and sultanas.

We had the Humber serviced three times per annum each year.

Mother never went short of housekeeping.

She had an account at Atkinson-Sievewright's.

She paid two visits per annum each year to her unmarried cousin at Bispham first class on the LMS, and father never knew what it was to miss the Old Trafford Test.

That's what I call the respectable North.

The Southerners don't know it exists, do they?

They think the North consists entirely of tripe and onions, the Rovers Return, flat caps and whippets, unemployment and Bill Maynard and his disgusting belly.

It wouldn't be so bad, if he could act, would it?

It's people like him who give the North a bad name.

Any road, why should I bother to defend it?

There's no need.

It stands up to criticism, does the North.

Am I right?

I am.

I tell you this, though – I'm dreading this trip to London.

It gives me the pip, does London.

All those Arabs with their cataracts and their wives with hairy legs.

What are they doing living in England?

What about our boys?

No wonder there's a housing shortage.

They wouldn't have them living in the North, I tell you.

We're particular about things like that.

That's why I'm dreading this visit.

I'm only doing it to please Hallam.

As far as I'm concerned the South is rubbish.

Utter rubbish.

The taxi drew up into the station forecourt.

Mrs Place alighted and paid the driver his fare.

She summoned a porter, who established her luggage on his trolley and invited her to follow him to the ticket barrier.

'Going to London, missus?' he said.

'That's right,' said Mrs Place.

'My sympathies.'

High above the city a skein of geese flying southwards called softly to each other.

Chapter Two

It was a High Speed Train.

The wistful lady with the tight-belted burberry and the long, elegant legs stared at its snarling, sneering front.

She smiled her wistful smile.

Softly she said to herself under her breath:

'You're so aggressive, high speed train. Fierce. Sneering. Snarling. So arrogant.

'You remind me of him.'

She smiled her wistful smile once more.

She reached out and began to stroke the snarling, sneering yellow snout of the high speed train.

'And you're handsome, too, high speed train,' she said to herself. 'Yes, my dear. Yes, you *are* like him.'

The guard blew his whistle.

'Low key lady on high speed train,' said the lady to herself.

She smiled.

And she said out loud:

'I like it – low key lady on high speed train.'

A porter shouted at her.

He opened the door of the carriage and she stepped inside and with a hiss and shiver of its flanks the train set off for London.

I do like company when I travel, don't you?

Well, it helps pass the time.

Am I right?

I am.

There's that lady sat the other end of the compartment in the white burberry.

It's a very expensive burberry, is that.

I saw one just like it in Atkinson-Sievewright's three Saturdays since and it cost all of one hundred and fifty guineas.

I'm going to talk to her.

Well, as I told you before – I am an extremely nosey person, and I don't care who knows it.

Anyway, it's unhealthy sitting on your own.

And I bet she's got a story to tell, too.

Even if she hasn't, I'll wheedle something out of her.

I'm going across to talk to her.

The high speed train snuffled its way out of the northern city.

It wormed over high, chill viaducts. It wriggled through soot-black, brick-lined cuttings. It slithered over chattering points.

Kay Washbrook, the wistful lady in the burberry, looked up from her magazine and saw, approaching her, a small lady with a tight mouth.

'Oh God,' she said to herself. 'She's coming to sit with me. Oh God Almighty.'

The small lady sat at the seat opposite her and rested her large maroon leather handbag on the table.

'My name's Mrs Place,' she said. 'Do you mind if I join you?'

The train picked up speed.

It sloughed off the suburbs. It hit the open countryside with a roar. And the high, bleak moorland crags looked down on it icily as it hissed along the river valley.

Kay Washbrook leaned back in her seat and closed her eyes.

On and on and on and on.

Dear God, how that woman could talk.

'. . . course, I don't think singing's been the same since Shirley Abicair and her zither. Am I right? I am. Mind you,

Alma Cogan had got a lot to recommend her. What about that Mary O'Hara? Whoever told her she could sing wants shooting out of hand. And as for . . .'

On and on and on.

Will they be expecting me?

Will he be there?

What will he look like after all this time?

Fifteen years.

I haven't seen him for fifteen years.

'. . . and don't tell me the victims don't know beforehand they're going to be on "This Is Your Life". Course they know. You can see it on their faces. Bob Monkhouse knew months before he was going to be on. He'd been rehearsing that crying for weeks. And as for . . .'

On and on and on.

They'll think I won't dare show up to the wedding.

Low key ladies don't do things like that, they'll say.

She won't turn up.

She won't dare.

She hasn't got the guts.

That's what they'll say, Harry and Hilary.

'. . . and can you tell me what's so funny about Cannon and Ball? I'm damned if I can see it. It's the same with Little and Large. The fat one's not so bad. But the skinny one's rubbish. And as for . . .'

On and on and on and on.

Dear God, how she rabbits.

She's not listening to a word I'm saying.

She's sat back in her seat with her eyes closed and a wistful sort of smile on her face.

It's very rude.

I don't approve.

I'm only trying to be sociable.

I wonder what her background is.

I wonder how old she is.

Well, she must be comfortably off to be wearing a burberry like that.

It must have cost all of a hundred and fifty guineas must that burberry.

I saw one identical in Atkinson-Sievewright's three Saturdays ago, and it wasn't a penny under one hundred and fifty guineas.

And she's got a good handbag, too.

Early forties, I'd put her.

But she could be a bit older and well preserved.

She's lovely blonde hair. I like the style.

The manageress of the gas showrooms used to have her hair done like that, only she had it a bit longer and never kept it clean.

It's a real wistful smile, is that.

Sad.

I think she's had sadness in her life.

Her husband was probably killed.

He was probably coming home from a business engagement late in the evening, and he'll have had one too many, and his reflexes won't have been as good as they should have been, and he'll have skidded on the greasy road while turning a sharp bend, and he'll have hit the wall of a railway bridge and gone straight through it on to the rails below and killed himself stone dead.

Poor devil.

Mind you, he shouldn't have been drinking, should he?

On the other hand he could always have died of natural causes.

There's a lot of it about these days.

He might have run off with another woman.

Or he might suddenly have started dressing up in women's clothing.

Our butcher did.

Dirty devil.

On the other hand she might not be married at all.

Is she wearing a wedding ring?

No, she's not.

Course, she could always be divorced.

Mrs Ikin from the foot parlour is.

That's it.

I bet she's divorced.

But why's she going to London?

Don't worry.

I'll soon find out.

On and on and on.

'. . . and the Boy Scouts aren't all they used to be neither. When Hallam and Garfield were in the Boy Scouts they used to . . . What did you say you were going to London for?'

The voice was sharp.

Kay Washbrook opened her eyes with a start.

'Pardon?'

'I was asking you why you were going to London.'

'To see my daughter.'

'I beg your pardon? Do you think you could speak up a bit louder. You've got a habit of mumbling under your breath. If you open your mouth a bit wider, and breathe deeply before you speak, you'll find it makes all the difference. Now then, love. You were saying?'

Kay Washbrook smiled.

'I'm going to London to visit my daughter,' she said.

The train hooted and gobbled up a country station in a blur of stinging snow.

What did I tell you?

I knew I'd worm it out of her.

I bet her daughter's in the Wrens.

She looks the sort of woman who'd have a daughter in the Wrens.

You can tell them a mile off.

Like Roman Catholics.

They've got a look about them, have Roman Catholics, haven't they?

Not that I've got anything against Roman Catholics.

It's just that I can't stand their religion.

This train's going very fast.

I hope the driver's not drunk.

Well, you hear such stories, don't you?

And that woman with the hairy legs and the buck teeth's been up and down this carriage ever since we left the station.

I cannot stand people who walk up and down trains.

What is the necessity of it?

Answer me that.

Hello, she's closed her eyes again.

And she's smiling that smile.

She'll be thinking about her daughter.

If she's not in the Wrens, I wonder what she does for a living?

She could work in a bank.

Lots of people do.

Of course she could always be in prison and her mother's going to visit her, and that's why she looks so nervous about things.

She's not at ease, you know.

She's got that smile on her face, but she's twisting her fingers all the time and I can feel her feet tapping under the table, and, if I look hard enough, I can see a little pulse twitching in her neck.

She's got a lovely neck.

So smooth.

So white and elegant.

She's a very beautiful woman, is this one.

I wonder if her daughter's beautiful, too.

It doesn't always follow.

You'll very often find that beautiful women breed very ugly daughters.

Some of them are ashamed of it and don't want to be seen with them.

On the other hand, you get some who like to be seen with an ugly daughter.

It makes them seem all the more beautiful, you see.

It's human nature, is that.

I wonder if she's like that?

I wonder, I wonder.

I'm going to get to the bottom of this mystery, if it's the last thing I do.

On and on and on.

Dear God, she never stops.

'. . . she's here again. That woman with the buck teeth and the hairy legs. She can't have been gone a minute. Up and down. Up and down. I'm going to complain to the guard if this continues. And as for that fellow with toothbrush moustache and the flat feet, I've a good mind to . . .'

Kay Washbrook rubbed at the window with her glove and looked out.

The moorland crags had been left behind, and the hills were rounded and rolling.

The snow lay heavy on the fields, criss-crossed by the tracks of small and frightened animals.

A squat manor house fluttered with fantail pigeons.

A small girl muffled up against the cold in a bright red anorak waved at the train.

Kay Washbrook raised her arm slightly.

Hilary.

Fifteen years since I've seen her.

She was a little girl.

Now she's a grown woman.
How beautiful she will be.
And Harry?
Will he be as handsome as ever?
She felt a tug at her sleeve.
She turned to face Mrs Place.

'I'm not being nosey, but is there anything upsetting you? I mean, is everything all right with your daughter that you're going to visit? I don't mind talking about it, you know, if you feel it'll make things better. These things are often better out than in, you know. Am I right? I am.'

Go on, Kay.
Tell her.
Tell the nosey old bat.

Kay Washbrook smiled broadly at her travelling companion.

'I haven't seen my daughter for fifteen years,' she said.
'I'm divorced.
'The judge took my daughter off me.
'He said I was an unfit mother.
'He said she was to live with her father.
'I haven't seen my daughter for fifteen years.
'I haven't seen her father for fifteen years.'
So there.
Put that in your pipe and smoke it.

Well, would you credit it?
Fancy.
I told you she wasn't all she was cracked up to be.
Am I right?
I am.

Chapter Three

The high speed train with the low key lady sped ever southwards, preening the ribbons of rails as it curved through the city with its damp brown buses and its sullen brick terraced houses.

Black-headed gulls wheeled over a rubbish dump.

Swans skidded squatly on an ice-covered canal. Pied wagtails flickered and flittered on the margins of a sewerage farm. Tufted duck and pochard bobbed on a thin-lipped reservoir.

Faster and faster and faster.

These high speed trains are all very well, but what about the people who run them?

The guard's a blackie for a start off.

I mean, I know that lots are clever in their own way, but has he been over long enough to understand the signals?

I think I'll have a dressed crab sandwich.

She's still got her eyes closed, that one.

A divorcee, eh?

Not that I've got anything against divorce as such.

Some of my closest friends have been involved in divorce proceedings.

There's the lady I buy my corn plasters from, Mrs Ikin from the Foot and Beauty Department at Maison Enid's.

Well, she's been divorced twice, has Mrs Ikin.

And a nicer woman you couldn't possibly wish to meet.

Clean?

She's spotless.

I wonder if she'd like one of my sandwiches?

They're very nice.

They've got the crusts cut off and I used real butter.

'No, thank you.'

Kay Washbrook shook her head when Mrs Place offered her one of her sandwiches.

'Are you sure?' said Mrs Place.

'Quite sure,' said Kay Washbrook.

'Well, would you like a potted meat sandwich instead?' said Mrs Place, opening another packet of sandwiches.

Kay Washbrook shook her head and closed her eyes once more.

Munch, munch, munch.

At least it stopped her talking.

What were they doing now, Harry and Hilary?

Nervous fingers clawed at her gut. The palms of her hands began to sweat. The pulse in her neck began to throb.

Oh God, why did I ever agree to go to this wedding?

I was happy.

I was contented.

And now I'm in turmoil.

Come on, high speed train.

Do your stuff.

Please, please, please.

Break down.

I don't want to go to this wedding.

There was no snow in London.

Hilary sat in front of her dressing table in her flat in Wimbledon.

Her long golden hair was pinned back with a green elastic band as she applied make-up to her face.

'I bet she doesn't come,' she said to her reflection in the mirror.

'I know it. She won't come.'

She pursed her lips and carefully outlined them with her brush.

'But what, if she does? What will I say to her? Will I kiss her? Will I shake her hand?'

A small pulse in her neck began to throb.

In his apartment some ten miles away Harry brushed a speck of dust from the lapel of his silver grey suit.

He tightened the knot in his pure silk navy blue tie.

He went into the bedroom.

His second wife Peggy sat at the dressing table, naked to the waist.

She did not see him enter.

Her breasts were large. The nipples were rosy pink.

He stood silently at the door.

Will she come, he said to himself.

Will she, will she?

He tiptoed up to his second wife and stood behind her.

He placed his hands on her breasts and squeezed them gently. She leaned back and pressed her head into his groin.

'Jesus, Harry,' she said. 'You smell like a feckin' brothel.'

The high speed began to slow.

The heart beat of the low key lady began to quicken.

He's stopping.

He's going to stop.

Good old high speed train.

Break down.

Don't take me to the wedding.

'This train's stopping.'

Kay Washbrook opened her eyes and stared at Mrs Place who was rubbing the window furiously with the wrapping which had contained the packet of dressed crab sandwiches.

'This train's slowing down,' she said. 'What time's your wedding?'

'Half past two,' said Kay Washbrook, and the train jerked

as the driver applied the brakes more fiercely.

'Half two? Well, you're cutting it very fine, aren't you? I mean, this train isn't due in till 13.25 and if there are any delays . . . Where are you going to for this wedding?'

'Wimbledon,' said Kay Washbrook, and immediately wished she hadn't told the mean-lipped woman, who launched into an account of the life and times of her elder son, Hallam, who also by chance happened to live in Wimbledon and had written scripts for Dick Emery, though he considered Terry and June total rubbish.

'We'll share a cab to Wimbledon. I know the way slightly so I'll be able to direct the driver,' said Mrs Place. 'I'd have got the earlier train, if I was you. You see, if this train breaks down or gets held up at signals or . . .'

Shut up.

Shut up, shut up.

I don't want to go to the wedding.

I must have been mad to say I would.

I'm happy in my own home, totally on my own, low key and contented.

Why spoil it?

Go on, train.

Stop, stop, stop.

'It's picking up speed.'

'Pardon?'

'The train. It's picking up speed. You're in luck. Have a dressed crab sandwich.'

Kay Washbrook stood up.

'Will you excuse me for a moment?'

'I beg your pardon?'

'I need to go to the toilet.'

Mrs Place fixed her with accusing eyes as she squeezed her way out into the corridor.

'You know where it is, do you?'

Kay Washbrook nodded.

'Well, take a tip from me. Wipe the seat with your hankie before you sit down. You can't be too careful these days.

'I remember we once went on a coach tour of Yugoslavia and there was this great pudding of a woman sat on the front seat next to the courier.

'I don't think she'd shaved her armpits for five years . . .'

'I'm sorry,' said Kay Washbrook. 'I've got to go.'

She lurched down the corridor. She opened the door of the toilet. She closed it behind her. She leaned against it and sighed with relief.

And then a great welling of nausea overwhelmed her and she staggered to the wash basin and was violently sick.

The high speed train swayed as it picked up speed and thrust its yellow snout Londonwards.

She doesn't look too good to me.

It'll be nerves.

It'll be . . .

There she does it again – the woman with the buck teeth and the hairy legs.

It's disgusting.

I'm not a prejudiced woman, but people like that I'd have put up against a wall and shot by the Foreign Legion in those funny hats with the white things hanging down the back.

Do you remember Beau Geste?

It was a good film, was Beau Geste.

So was that one with Laurel and Hardy.

I think it was called Beau Chumps.

I took mother to see it at the Criterion Kinema.

We had a quarter pound box of Dairy Milk and a packet of chocolate dragees and mother . . .

I'm wandering again.

I wonder what she's up to in the toilets?

I wonder if she's all right.

I'll give her five minutes then I'll go and knock on the door and see if she wants any assistance.

Fancy having her daughter taken from her.

It makes you think.

Am I right?

I am.

Well, it must have been serious for the judge to have awarded custody to the father.

Maybe, she was a child-batterer, or a heavy drinker.

It's always the quiet ones, who are the deepest, isn't it?

My cousin, Marion, was a case in point.

You wouldn't think butter would melt in her mouth, yet one day without warning she upped and off and ran away with the man who serviced the mobile library.

This train's picking up speed again.

I hope the driver's got a happy home life.

We don't want him wondering what his wife's up to when his back's turned, when he should be looking out for the signals.

There's a lot of that about.

I'll give her another two minutes, then I'll go and see if she's okay.

Kay Washbrook sat on the toilet, her head between her knees, her blonde hair streaked across her brow, her knees quivering weakly.

The motion of the fast-moving train threw her from side to side and she was forced to cling to the handle to keep herself from falling to the floor.

'Kay, Kay,' she said out loud.

'What a shambles. What a state I'm in.

'Kay Washbrook, you are a mess.

'Kay Washbrook, why ever did you get on this train?

'Kay Washbrook, what is to become of you?

'Oh God, oh God.'

The train roared through a tunnel.

* * *

Harry Washbrook, ex-husband of Kay, sat in the front seat of the Alfa Romeo Sud.

Next to him sat his second wife, Peggy.

She was driving.

They were crawling behind a clucking milk float on the Ridgeway of Wimbledon.

'Get a fecking move on,' said Peggy.

And Harry Washbrook winced inwardly.

She would be on the train now.

Low key lady on high speed train.

Why had she accepted the invitation? God damnit, it didn't make sense. Why had Hilary invited her? He'd argued with her. He'd pleaded with her. No. She was adamant. Her mother must come to the wedding.

And secretly, when his daughter had said that, he had felt a flow of pleasure.

By God, he was excited.

He could feel it in every bone and in every fibre.

'She won't come, you know.'

He jumped a little.

'What?'

'Your ex-wife. She'll chicken out. She'll be at home now, sticking pins in wax effigies of you and Hilary.'

She laughed her familiar bronchial laugh and coughed her familiar smoker's cough.

She rested her hand lightly on his knee and squeezed it, and inwardly he recoiled, and he knew she sensed it, and he was not displeased.

They turned into the road where Hilary lived with Leo, the young man she was to marry.

They pulled up outside the house.

A viburnum bloomed pink in the front garden as they walked down the path. The berries on the pyracantha were fiery red. A blackbird clacked angrily in the undergrowth of a soot-soaked holly.

Leo answered the door and led them upstairs to the flat.

'Hilary's just finishing getting togged up,' he said.

'Sure,' said Peggy. 'We have whisky?'

'We have whisky,' said Leo with a grin, and he poured her a large measure.

She downed it in a single gulp and held out her glass for more.

Leo grinned.

Harry Washbrook winced.

Then the door of the bedroom opened and Hilary stepped out.

'Wow!' said Leo.

'Hilary,' said Harry Washbrook. 'You look beautiful.'

'Kay Washbrook. You look ugly.

'You look old and you look ugly and you look careworn and, above all, you look petrified.'

Kay Washbrook talked to herself as she combed out her hair and repaired the makeup on her face in the mirror.

Someone knocked on the door.

'Go away. It's engaged,' she cried out.

'It's me,' said Mrs Place.

'Oh Lord,' said Kay Washbrook.

'Are you all right in there? Do you need assistance?'

'I'm fine, thank you.'

'What's that? Will you speak up? I can't hear you. Open your mouth. Breathe in deeply. And speak clearly.'

Oh, God.

Go away.

Go a-way, you interfering, old bat.

The handle of the door was rattled violently.

'Listen,' shouted Mrs Place. 'I'm going to fetch the guard. Can you understand me? I'm going to fetch the guard to break open the lock. Now don't go away, will you?'

Kay Washbrook opened the door of the toilet and stepped outside into the corridor.

'I'm fine,' she said. 'Just fine.'

Mrs Place looked her up and down and sniffed hard.

'Well, you don't look it to me,' she said.

She doesn't neither.

Look at her sat there staring out of the window.

Her face is peeky.

She's got bags under her eyes.

It's malnutrition.

I've read about it in the papers.

Women, when they get to that certain age, and they've no family living at home to support them, start to neglect their food.

They don't neglect their appearances.

It's just that they don't eat.

If only she'd have a dressed crab sandwich, she'd be as right as rain.

She could half my Mars Bar, if she wished.

They're very nourishing, are Mars Bars.

I prefer Bounty myself, but Mrs Tattersall at the corner shop was right out, when I called in this morning.

Mind you, that's nothing new.

Last week there wasn't a tin of Ambrosia creamed rice in the establishment and . . .

On and on and on.

Yakky Northern lady.

Yakky, yakky, yakky.

How do you do it?

'. . . the thing was I'd set my heart on a tin of Ambrosia creamed rice for my afters. I'd got a lovely jar of damson jam our Hazel, that's my son Garfield's wife, had made last back end, and I was really looking forward to putting a blob on my rice pudding and dunking it with maids of honour and then . . . is this train slowing down again?'

She looked out of the window with her eyes flashing.

'It is,' she said. 'It's slowing down. We're not scheduled to stop, are we?'

'It might be signals,' said Kay Washbrook. 'They might be against us.'

'Well, they've no right to go against us,' said Mrs Place. 'Isn't that typical of British Railways? You pay through the nose for a first class ticket, and they go and put the signals against you. Of course, that lot in second class couldn't care less. Typical of them. You'll find most of them are squaddies with boils on the backs of their necks. It's the soap they use, you know.

'It's stopped.

'It has.

'This train's stopped.'

It had indeed.

It stood still and silent.

Kay Washbrook smiled to herself.

High speed train.

So handsome.

So sleek and silky.

High speed train, I adore you.

Chapter Four

Harry Washbrook stood in the living room of Hilary's flat.

He had his arm around her waist.

He motioned with his head towards his second wife, Peggy, who was halfway through her fourth whisky.

'It's started already,' he said.

'Shush,' said Hilary. 'There's nothing you can do about it. Half an hour's time, and she'll be well and truly plastered.'

'Oh God,' said Harry Washbrook. 'I've enough on my plate without all of that.'

'Are you nervous?'

'Yes. Are you?'

'Petrified,' said Hilary. 'Do you think she'll come?'

'I don't know.'

'Do you want her to come?'

Harry Washbrook turned his daughter to face him.

'Yes,' he said. 'Very much.'

And then he drew her into him and hugged her fiercely.

'Oh God, I'm longing for it,' he said.

Don't move, high speed train.

Stay just where you are.

High speed train, do not, I implore you, get me to the church on time.

Mrs Place stabbed at the window with her right forefinger.

'Well, that's ominous,' she said. 'It's the guard walking down the track. He's a blackie, too. Typical. They think they can get away with murder, just because they've got lovely white teeth. Get a move on, man.'

Kay Washbrook looked out of the window beyond the

track and the signal wires and the new concrete sleepers lying astride the embankment's lip.

'What a lovely spot,' she said.

'I beg your pardon?' said Mrs Place.

'It's a lovely spot. Lock gates. Black and white cattle. I love canals.'

'I beg your pardon?' said Mrs Place.

'Canals. They're so beautiful. So slow. So unhurried. Everything's too quick these days. Everything happens so suddenly. I was born in the wrong age. Stage coaches. That's the way to travel. Stopping overnight in inns with great cobbled courtyards and encrusted with vines. Nice and slow. Nice and slow and long.'

She sighed nice and slow and long.

The intercom crackled. Someone coughed. And then a voice spoke.

'This is your guard speaking. We apologize for the hold up and the ensuing delay, but we have a train broken down further along the line. As soon as we have any further information, we shall let you know and inform you. Thank you.'

Perfect.

Just perfect.

Oh, high speed train, I love you.

I adore you. I worship you.

There's something fishy about her, you know.

Am I right?

I am.

She's supposed to be bursting her boilers to get to her daughter's wedding and yet the train's stopped here stone dead and she doesn't turn a hair.

She looks pleased, in fact.

She looks delighted.

Canals!

Stage coaches.

You know what she just said?

She said – I wonder who lives in that lock keeper's cottage?

She said – I wonder if that woman who was feeding the hens in the gardens has a loving, tender husband, and I wonder what he does for a living.

Well, I can tell her that straight off.

He'll be on the social security.

They all are these days.

This country's developed into a nation of skivers.

He'll be living in that cottage rent free, stopping in bed all morning till the pubs open and he can spend his social security on booze, and then he'll be into the bookies, and then it's back home to bed till tea time, and then up he gets and out to the pub supping all night with all the other skivers.

You can't tell me anything about him.

I know his sort only too well.

Scum.

That's what he is.

Scum.

On and on and on.

How I hate Northern women.

Coarse.

Malignant, narrow-minded, shrewish, selfish, ungenerous.

How I hate their malice.

How I hate their vicious nosiness.

Mrs Place leaned forward and wagged her finger in front of Kay Washbrook's face.

'And she'll be no better than him neither,' she said. 'She'll be selling those hens' eggs for money and not declaring it to the social security.

'I've a good mind to report her. Not that it'll do any good. You can't teach people like that a lesson. Scum – that's what they are. They live off fish and chips and they breed like rabbits. She'll have a fancy man you know. Oh yes, she's forced to have a fancy man.'

'I had a fancy man once,' said Kay Washbrook.

Mrs Place sat back in her seat suddenly.

Her mouth sagged open.

'I beg your pardon?' she said.

Ah, look at her nostrils quiver. Look at the spikes of malice in the eye. The Northern lady hovers for the kill.

'Did I hear right?' said Mrs Place. 'Did I hear you say you had a fancy man?'

'Yes,' said Kay Washbrook.

'Fancy.'

Ah, see the jut of the bosom. See the tightening of the jaw. Nosey Northern lady waits to pounce.

How I hate Northern women.

How I despise them.

'You're dying to know all about it, aren't you?'

Mrs Place's neck flushed.

'Well, I wouldn't go as far as to . . .' she said, and her voice trailed off in a cough and a splutter.

'You're dying to know why I haven't seen my daughter for fifteen years, aren't you?' said Kay Washbrook, and before Mrs Place could reply, she continued: 'You're dying to know why they took her away from me, when my husband divorced me. You're dying to know why I'm going to the wedding, aren't you? Aren't you just?'

Mrs Place fingered the collar of her blouse.

'Well, I can't say I've not been interested,' she said. 'I mean to say, I don't want to appear nosey. I don't want you to upset yourself going over old history. But as I always say getting things off your chest can be . . . well, it can, can't it?'

Kay Washbrook smiled at her.

'Sit back,' she said. 'And I'll tell you.'

There was a jerk and a creak.

And slowly the train began to move forwards.

In London the sun was shining.

It was low in the sky. It was weak.

But it was shining.

It sent watery shafts through the window of Hilary's flat and lit upon the face of Peggy.

Her face was flushed, and her voice was loud.

'Can somebody tell me why I ever married her?' said Harry Washbrook.

'Daddy. No,' said Hilary. 'Not on my wedding day.'

'I must have been mad.'

'Daddy, please.'

Peggy broke into a bout of coughing. Dribbles of liquid appeared in her nostrils. Her cheeks went scarlet. Her chest heaved.

'What time is your mother arriving?'

Hilary shook her head.

'I don't know. She didn't say.'

Harry Washbrook squeezed tightly at his daughter's hand.

'Low key lady on high speed train,' he said. 'I like that.'

'Low key lady, they used to call me,' said Kay Washbrook. 'Kay's so placid, they used to say. She's so low key. Nothing gets her down. Nothing gets her excited. She's always the same. A loving wife. A loving mother. Never changes.

'They were right.

'And so I thought to myself one day – right then, I'll change. I'll go off the rails.'

'Fancy,' said Mrs Place. 'I say.'

Kay Washbrook smiled again.

The train hummed.

High speed train blurring the trees and the fields and the spires of churches and the towers of timbered manor houses.

High speed train speeding to London.

What's wrong with me?

What's happened to the low key lady I left at the station an hour ago?

I want to go to London.

I want to see him.

Is he as handsome as ever? Is he as loving as ever? Is he as secure?

I'm petrified of going to London.

Stop now, high speed train.

No, carry on.

'And so I got myself a lover,' said Kay Washbrook.

'Fancy,' said Mrs Place.

'It was so easy. I couldn't believe how easy it was.'

'Fancy.'

Northern lady, how I hate you. Mean. Oozing with malice.

Nosey, nosey, Northern lady.

'Yes, I got myself a lover,' said Kay Washbrook. 'He wasn't very special. He wasn't even very keen.'

'Fancy,' said Mrs Place. 'And did you . . . well, you know, did you?'

'Oh yes. We went to bed.'

'Fancy.'

'He was shy. I was passionate. It was frightening. The things I did. The things I said.'

It's always the same with these deep ones, you know.

They look as though butter wouldn't melt in their mouth.

You take my Auntie Medora, for example.

Well, she was a . . .

There she goes again, the woman with the buck teeth and the hairy legs.

Either she's got a very weak bladder or she's supping double gins and tonics at the buffet.

Of course she might be . . .

As I say, it's always the deep ones who've got the most to hide.

The things she's telling me about what she got up to with this lover of hers.

Quite shameless she is.

So specific about the details.

That's the whole trouble with the world these days – people are too specific.

Take the telly, for example.

What about that Andrea Newman.

Disgusting.

All those bare breasts.

Well, we all know women have got bosoms, don't we?

There's no need to set them to music on the television with all that heaving and grunting in bed and men's bums going up and down.

It's disgusting.

Am I right?

I am.

'I was quite blatant about the affair, you know.'

'Fancy.'

'We went to the local pictures together. He took me to country pubs in his car. We went to dances. I wanted to be found out.'

'And were you?'

'No.'

'So what did you do?'

'I got myself another lover.'

A roar and a rattle as a northbound high speed train flung itself at their slip stream.

Chapter Five

Two hours to the wedding.

The sun still shone in London.

Leo propped himself against the mantelpiece and sang.

'If I was the marrying kind, which thank the Lord I'm not, sir.

'The type of man that I would wed would be a . . .'

Peggy quaffed.

Hilary stifled a sob and rushed into her bedroom.

Harry Washbrook followed her.

She lay on the bed sobbing.

He rested his hand diffidently on her golden hair.

'Get me a tissue,' she said. 'They're on the dressing table.'

He went to the dressing table. There was a picture there in a silver frame.

'How long have you had this picture of your mother?' he said.

'Not long,' said Hilary. 'She sent it to me after I'd invited her to the wedding.'

She watched her father as he examined the picture in the weak shafts of the winter sunshine.

'She's rather beautiful, isn't she?' she said.

'Do you know when this was taken?' said Harry Washbrook.

'No.'

'It was taken the year I discovered she'd been unfaithful. She'd been having affairs right left and centre. She'd be . . .'

He paused and he arched his eyebrows.

'Yes,' he said. 'She is rather beautiful.'

And then the door burst open and Peggy burst open. She

lurched towards him.

'What have you got there?' she rasped.

He tried to hide the picture.

'It's her,' she said. 'It's her picture. Give it to me. I want it.'

'Peggy,' he said. 'For heaven's sake, behave yourself.'

'I want it. Give me that fecking picture.'

She lashed out at him with her fist. She staggered against him and clawed at his collar.

He slapped her hard against her cheek, and very slowly she slumped to the floor at his feet.

He looked down on her, and on his face was an expression of utter loathing.

'I'll never forget his face when I told him of my affair,' said Kay Washbrook. 'Loathing. Real loathing. I'd never ever seen such loathing.'

The snow was patchy now.

There were meadows full of Friesian cattle. Villages nestled in hollows of low wooded hills. Pheasants scuttled low over spiky pastures.

'He didn't say a thing. He stared at me. He stared at me and he stared and he stared.'

A branch line curved away through a narrow cutting littered with rubble. A grey-bricked warehouse. A gap-roofed engine shed. An impatient level crossing.

'And my daughter was there while all this was going on. She was in the room. She was lying on the bed sobbing her heart out. Her whole body heaved. I'd never seen such unhappiness. I'd never seen such total misery.

'And I didn't feel a thing.'

Mrs Place took another bite from her potted meat sandwich.

'The driver's making up time,' she said.

'Suddenly he scooped her up in his arms,' said Kay Washbrook. 'He took her downstairs. He drove off in his car. And that's the last I ever saw of her.'

'Fancy.'

'He came back a few days later. He packed up all his clothes. He packed up all her clothes. And all he said was: "Keep out of my way." I did. I went out in the garden, and I dead-headed the roses.

'Only some of them weren't dead.

'How about that for a low key lady?'

Peggy lay on the floor of the bedroom, snoring.

Suddenly Hilary heaved herself off the bed and threw herself into her father's arms.

He hugged her tightly.

She sobbed uncontrollably.

After a while she said:

'When I was small, you never hugged me. You never held me tight in your arms like this.

'You never showed me any passion.'

'In bed there was no passion from him,' said Kay Washbrook. 'There was no warmth. He took me every night. Every night without fail. Sometimes he waited for me. Sometimes he didn't.'

The lady with the protruding teeth and the hairy legs passed down the carriage, but this time Mrs Place ignored her.

'Can you understand what it was like?' said Kay Washbrook. 'Can you?'

Mrs Place licked her lips.

'We're slowing down again,' she said.

'Yes,' said Kay Washbrook.

'I can feel the brakes.'

'Yes.'

'It's nice to know they're working, isn't it?'

'Yes.'

I was beautiful then.

Everyone said I was beautiful.

Everyone said he was handsome. We were a handsome couple.

So what happened?

Why did the low key lady change?

Boredom, was it? Thirst for adventure?

I was so low key.

Why did I change so suddenly?

After all this time I still don't know.

There's no answer to it.

The train wailed mournfully at a distant signal and reduced its speed more and more.

It's the daughter I feel sorry for.

It's always the children who suffer most.

Am I right?

I am.

Poor little mite.

She must have been devastated by it.

I wonder if she knew the man her mother had been having an affair with.

It could have been her father's best friend.

What a disgrace.

On the other hand it could have been the insurance collector. It very often is. Mind you, if she paid by banker's order, she wouldn't have had the opportunity. She looks to me as though she'd choose a much younger man to have an affair with. The teenage son of her own best friend. That's it. What a disgrace. She should be thoroughly ashamed of herself. She's ruined his chances of going to university. Well, with all the canoodling and stuff going on in secret assignations he'd have no time to do his swatting and his exam results would be forced to suffer, wouldn't they? It wouldn't do his spotty face any good neither. Isn't it dreadful the way young people get covered in spots these days? I think it's all the artificial preservatives you get in food. I think it's disgusting. If God had meant things to be preserved, He'd have put in artificial preservatives Himself when He first created them, wouldn't He? Well, He's like that, is God. He thinks of everything. And He's omniscient, too.

Am I right?

I am.

'Get out,' screamed Hilary at the top of her voice. 'Out, out, out.'

Leo stood at the door of her bedroom grinning sheepishly.

'Steady on,' he said. 'Cool it, eh?'

Hilary picked up one of Peggy's shoes which lay by the side of the recumbent, snoring body and hurled it with all her might at Leo.

He ducked and raising his arms in surrender backed out of the door and shut it behind him.

'Out, out, out,' screamed Hilary and she flung herself on to the bed once more and commenced tearing at the sheets.

Harry Washbrook stood stock still and watched her.

'All I remember of my daughter is her temper,' said Kay Washbrook.

'Fancy,' said Mrs Place.

'She was born with a vicious temper,' said Kay Washbrook. 'It was deep inside her soul like a malignant growth.'

'Fancy,' said Mrs Place. 'The guard's out on the track again.'

'She had this piercing scream,' said Kay Washbrook. 'And, even worse, she had this thin little wail of utter, total misery that would go on and on and on.'

'Fancy,' said Mrs Place. 'I wish that guard wouldn't

scratch his bottom like that in full view of the train.'

'Everything seemed to make her angry,' said Kay Washbrook. 'You could never please her. She always found fault. A new toy. A new dress. A special treat. You could see her fighting herself to deny the pleasure in her eyes. And she'd find fault. And there'd be tantrums and screams. And she'd rampage through the house tearing things to shreds.

'My God, you can't imagine the relief when he took her away.'

Harry Washbrook sat on the bed and held his daughter, Hilary, in his arms.

'Why on earth did I invite her to the wedding?' said Hilary, snuffling back the tears.

'That I do not know,' said her father.

'Fifteen years and not a peep out of her. No letters, no birthday cards. Nothing. Not a single solitary line of communication from her since the day you took me away, yet I write and ask her to my wedding. Why?'

'Because you're so fecking nosey.'

They turned sharply.

Peggy was hauling herself to her feet, clawing at the bed sheets and scrabbling at the carpet with her stocking feet.

Her lipstick was awry. Her hair was tossed and streaked. Her large bosom was streaked with stale whisky and cigarette ash.

'You're like all Northern women my dear,' said Peggy, dragging herself upright. 'You're fecking nosey. And you're fecking malicious.'

'Peggy!' said Harry Washbrook.

'You invited her, my dear, for one simple reason. Malice. You wanted to set her up with your father again,' said Peggy, and she cackled her bronchial cackle and swayed on her feet.

'Peggy, for heaven's sake,' said Harry Washbrook.

'Jayney mackers, what a game,' said Peggy. 'Mother and

father together again on the wedding day and all lovey dovey.

'What a fecking . . . what a . . . I'm going to be sick.'

She reeled out of the bedroom, her cheeks bulging, her shoulders heaving.

They heard the splat of her vomit as it hit the side of the wash basins. And then they heard her groan.

Hilary sank back on to the bed.

Harry Washbrook picked up the picture of his former wife, Kay, and looked at it.

'Low key lady,' he said softly. 'Low key lady smiling a low key smile. She looked just like that the day I found out about her affairs. She didn't deny a thing when I challenged her. She didn't say a word. She just smiled. That low key smile.

'That low key smile.

'A vague smile.

'Nothing behind it.

'Vague eyes.

'Nothing behind them.

'That was what incensed me, Hilary. I was furious about her affairs. I was livid. But that could have been sorted out. God damnit, I'd been having a bit on the side with Peggy for years.

'But that smile.

'It was that bloody smile that brought out all the loathing.

'That's why I snatched you up and drove off with you.

'It was that low key smile.'

He hurled the picture on to the bed.

Hilary did not open her eyes.

'And you, Hilary?' said Harry Washbrook. 'When I snatched you out of the house you screamed and you screamed and you screamed.

'Dreadful.

'I yelled at you. I threatened you with the palm of my hand. I shook you.

'Nothing.

'And then do you know what I did?

'I said very quietly: "It's all right. I'm taking you away from your mother. You'll never ever see her again."

'And in an instant you stopped. And I never saw that temper again until just now with Leo. Amazing.'

Hilary opened her eyes and smiled at her father.

'It must have been that smile that sparked you off,' said Harry Washbrook. 'It must have been the first thing you saw the day you were born.

'It must have been the first thing you saw every morning when she took you from the cot. It was the last thing you saw when she tucked you up at night.

'No wonder you had that temper.

'A low key smile.

'It's enough to drive you out of your mind.'

That smile of hers.

It's weird.

It looks so gentle and so harmless.

Yet behind it, well . . . behind it it's as though there's a madman peering out and gibbering at you.

Do you remember those Italian Prisoners of War they kept in those camps on the Moss?

Well, we used to go and watch them on Sunday mornings for something to do, and there was this one poor fellow and he used to grab hold of the wires really tightly and he'd just look at you and burst out laughing hysterically, yet when you looked at him his eyes were all gentle and content, and sometimes they were cold and indifferent.

It's like her smile.

Look at it now.

We've come to a dead stop.

She's got no chance of getting to the wedding.

And yet she's smiling.

It doesn't make sense.

Am I right?

I am.

Look at her – mean-mouthed, nosey, Northern lady.

My God, I've given her something to feast on.

Smile at her.

She can't understand it.

Smile again.

She turns her head away.

Good.

This train certainly chooses nice spots to stop at.

There's a heron flying to those woods over there. I love herons. I love the black shadows their wings cast over the water. I love the . . .

Fifteen years and not a word from her, and then suddenly she sends me an invitation to her wedding.

Why?

Why, why, why?

There's a green woodpecker. Look at the loop and sag of his flight. I love green woodpeckers. Yackle, yackle, yackle, they go. Lovely red crests they have. And I love the . . .

Why did I accept?

Why did I say I'd go?

Fifteen years without them, and I've been happy.

Why am I on this train?

Why, why?

'. . . so even if you don't get to the actual ceremony, at least you should be able to get to the reception. Don't worry. I'll get you there. I won't stand any old buck from the taxi driver. I'm not frightened of these darkies. If they want to live in this country, they've got to learn to abide by our rules. And one of our rules is that drivers should expect as part and parcel of their jobs to get a thorough sharacking from me, if they won't do their job properly.

'Am I right?

'I am.

'Now don't worry. I'll get you there in time to see your daughter in all her finery.'

'But that's not the point.'

'I beg your pardon?'

'It's not my daughter I want to see.

'It's him.

'It's my ex-husband I want to see.

'Come on, high speed train.

'Do your stuff.

'Come on, come on, come on.'

Chapter Six

With an icy roar and a snarl the high speed train blurred out of the tunnel.

Now it had reached the sunshine of the south country.

The snow was far behind.

The land was gentle.

It smiled a wistful smile.

Nearer and nearer and nearer. I wonder what he's feeling? Fear? Yes. Fear. He'll be terrified. Petrified.

'Not far to go now,' said Mrs Place. 'Now don't worry yourself about meeting your ex-husband. You're bound to be excited. But don't let it get on top of you. Breathe deeply and speak clearly when you first meet him. Don't let your excitement show.'

Excitement?

My dear woman, low ladies don't have emotions like that, my nosey, malicious, thin-lipped Northern crone.

'It's curiosity that's making you excited you see,' said Mrs Place. 'That's all it is – out and out curiosity.'

'Curiosity!' said Kay Washbrook.

Oh God, why did I speak to her?

It'll all come out in a flood now.

Yes, here we are. She's bracing herself for it. The jut of the jaw, the heave of the bosom, the licking of the lips, and here we go.

'You want to see how much he's aged. You want to gloat over him. You want to gloat at how he's been ravaged by time.

'And he will have been.

'Oh yes he'll be ravaged, love. Ravaged.'

She leaned forward intently and stared hard into Kay Washbrook's eyes and clasped both her wrists tightly.

Her voice was hard.

'You want to see the saggy cheeks and the creases at the corner of the mouth and the gravy stains on the front of his cardigan. You want to feast your eyes on his scrawny neck and the blue veins on the back of his hand. You want to look at him in his decline, and you want to gloat.

'Am I right?

'I am.'

Kay Washbrook removed her wrists from her grasp and looked out of the window.

'We're slowing down again,' she said softly.

Mrs Place grabbed hold of her wrists again and squeezed them so sharply that Kay Washbrook was compelled to turn round to face her again.

She saw two eyes burning with malice.

'It's my one big regret that my husband didn't live long enough to grow old and decrepit,' said Mrs Place.

'I used to sit and watch him when he was in his pomp and in his prime. He'd be polishing his bowls shoes, and he'd be humming softly to himself. And his brush would shick and shack over the leather. And his eyes would sparkle. And his flesh would glow. Shick, shack, shick, shack, went the brush on the leather and I'd think to myself—

'You wait.

'You just wait.

'You just wait till you grow old, you bugger.

'I'll have you then.'

'I'm growing old,' said Harry Washbrook. 'That's what's wrong with me – I'm growing old.'

He sat in the pink lloyd loom chair in Hilary's bedroom.

The sun was more intense now.

Hilary sat at the dressing table applying new make up to

her face and re-ordering her hair.

'I'm growing old,' said Harry Washbrook. 'And your mother won't have changed one jot.'

Hilary turned to him.

'No, daddy,' she said. 'You're young. You're handsome. You haven't changed one little scrap.'

'No,' said Harry Washbrook. 'No.'

'She's the one who'll have changed.'

Harry Washbrook shook his head and said softly once more:

'No. No.'

'Yes,' said Hilary fiercely. 'Yes, yes. She'll be an old woman, daddy. I can see her on the train now. An ageing Northern lady. A tight frizzy perm, she'll have.

'She'll be so proud of it, and it'll be pearly grey with tight, malignant little curls.

'But the rest of her?

'Shabby and old. She'll wear a shapeless woollen dress. Beige. She'll have a cardie. Light blue and acrylic. And her shoes'll be scuffed, and she'll use a compact with a cracked mirror, and there'll be lipstick on her teeth.

'And her face?

'Wrinkled and creased.

'I can see her face, daddy.

'It's the face of a tired, old, malicious Northern lady.'

There's not a wrinkle on her face, you know.

And her neck's smooth.

It's not scraggy like an old turtle.

She's still a very beautiful woman.

Her husband'll be mortified when he sees her.

They'll probably wheel him up to the station in a bathchair, and he'll have a perpetual dewdrop on the end of his nose, and he'll spill custard down his chin and he'll be forever fiddling with the buttons of his cardigan, and his flies'll be undone, and he'll not be able to speak proper, and he'll have that old man's smell of hollow chests and damp lungs.

On and on and on.

How does she do it?

The train's picking up speed again.

Oh God. Oh Lord.

'. . . and he'll be all old and scrawny and worn out . . .'

'No,' said Kay Washbrook. 'He won't be like that. He'll be as handsome as ever. He won't have changed one bit.'

'You must be joking,' said Mrs Place. 'Men change. It's one of the laws of nature, is that. They try to ignore it, do men. When they're in the full flood of their sex, they're so aggressive and arrogant about it. But how long does it last? Not long, love, not long. The sap runs dry and the stick begins to wither. And we know it, and they don't. Even while they're in their pomp and in their prime, us women can see it fading and flickering. And when it goes, it goes because it's eaten them alive. There's nothing left. Just a husk. He'll be an empty husk, will your husband.'

No, no, you nosey old Northern bat.

He'll have grown old gracefully.

And he'll have his regular lady.

He had a lady friend, when we were married. I never said a word to him, but I knew he had one. He'll be with her.

Maybe they're married.

I wonder what she's like.

Blonde and blowsy?

Small and mousey?

I wonder.

The high speed train reached the first fringes of the capital's sprawl.

And it screamed.

* * *

A flight of pintail crossed the elm-scratched horizon bound for the lake at Wimbledon Park.

A wren churred softly in the undergrowth.

Harry Washbrook looked out from the sitting room of his daughter's flat.

Hilary and her prospective bridegroom, Leo sat on the sofa.

She held his hand.

Peggy came out of the bedroom. In her hand was the photograph of Harry Washbrook's first wife.

She had washed her face. She had brushed her hair. She had scrubbed clean the whisky and cigarette ash stains on her chest. Her lipstick was bold.

'I'm sorry, Harry,' she said.

Harry Washbrook shrugged his shoulders.

'It's you who provoke me,' she said.

'Me?'

'I can't cope with it.'

'What can't you cope with?'

'Your looks.'

'My looks?' said Harry Washbrook. 'What the hell are you talking about?'

Peggy smiled. It was a weary smile.

'You haven't aged at all, Harry,' she said. 'You still look the same as the day I first met you.'

'Nonsense.'

'It isn't, it isn't,' said Peggy, and her voice was sharp. 'You're as handsome as ever, Harry. There's not an ounce of extra weight on you. There's no bald patches, no wrinkles, no creases. And will you ever look at the state of me?'

'You're still a beautiful woman, Peggy,' said Harry Washbrook.

She advanced across the room and stood in front of him, jutting up her chin and pressing her bosom into his chest.

'Look at me,' she said firmly. 'Look at me.'

Very slowly Harry Washbrook turned his face away from her.

'And now look at her,' said Peggy very softly, and she lifted up the photograph of Kay Washbrook and passed it in front of his eyes. 'She's a beautiful woman, and she won't have changed one bit, and you'll look a handsome couple.'

Hilary stood up from the sofa, brushing away Leo's restraining hand.

'Go fetch her,' said Peggy. 'The two of you. Go to the station and fetch her.'

Harry Washbrook looked at his daughter. Hilary returned his gaze with a slow arching of her eyebrows.

'For Christ's sake,' snapped Peggy. 'Go to the fecking station and fetch her.'

Silently Harry Washbrook and Hilary left the flat.

Peggy watched them from the window as they hurried hand in hand down the front path.

She turned to Leo.

'So what is going to become of us then?' she said.

Suburban gardens.

Dormant flowering cherries and weeping plums. Red holly of pyracantha, purple berries of berberis.

The high speed train roared past them, the scent of London deep in its snarling yellow snout.

Suburban parks.

Shoveller and black-headed gull. Flop-eared spaniel and loping labrador. Shale of tennis court. Nap of bowling green.

The high speed train brushed them aside with a scornful sneer.

On and on and on.

Is there no end to her?

'. . . you see, you've got to complain about everything. Take those little diamonds of processed cheese you buy in the supermarket. Can you get them out of their silver paper?

I can't. And I don't know anyone else who can. You try to peel the paper back, and all you get is cheese stuck under your fingernails. You try to cut them in half with a knife, and they just go all squelchy under the blade. And what do we do about it? I'll tell you. Nothing.

'Am I right?

'I am.

'It's the same with boiled sweets. Do you know, I've not had a decent boiled sweet since last Preston Guild. They're rubbish these days, are boiled sweets. Last time I had a decent boiled sweet was . . .'

Is that what I shall turn in to?

A nosey Northern woman.

Tight little mouth. Tight little bottom. Tight little eyes. Tight little brain.

I hate you, Northern lady.

I loathe you.

'. . . it's the same with the television. Complain. If you don't like a programme, complain to the authorities. I do. If I see that disgusting Marti Caine showing off her do-dahs one more time, I'll . . .'

Nosey. Narrow-gutted. Narrow-minded.

And so aggressive.

How I hate aggressive women.

How I hate positive women.

Be a low key lady all your life. Always give in with a low key smile. Shrug your shoulders. Smile again.

It's the only way to cope.

Low key and lonely.

'If you want to cope, you've got to be thoroughly unpleasant all your life. That's why women are nature's survivors – because we're so much more unpleasant than men.

'Am I right?

'I am.

'And that's why you're going to this wedding. You've been wondering why all the time, haven't you? Well I'll tell you. You're going so you can be thoroughly objectionable and unpleasant. You're going to ruin everyone's day. You're going to make it so horrendous, they'll never ever forget it for the rest of their lives. You're going to get your own back.

'Am I right?

'I am.'

'How long to go, daddy?'

'Ten minutes.'

'I'm so nervous.'

'So am I.'

The main line station.

The destination board flickers its eyelids. A diesel clatters. Its exhaust echoes. Its fumes are shrill and blue.

'I'm petrified of seeing her stepping off that train, daddy.'

'So am I.'

I'm not the least bit nervous now.

Low key lady once more.

How shall I cope with them, my daughter, her groom, my ex-husband, his regular lady?

Any way I like.

Like this, perhaps.

Hullo, my dears. What bliss to meet you. What enchantment. This is a bod I picked up on the train. Don't know his name, but he's rather gorgeous, don't you think?

Ah, you must be my daughter.

Enchanting, my dear.

And this is your young man, is it?

How nice what a sweetie.

And you?

You're Harry.

What a silly, boring suit you're wearing.

And what a silly, boring man, you are.

'He's slowing down. We must be coming near to the station. We are. There's the engine sheds. Come on then, love, we best be getting our luggage ready.'

Or I could make my entrance like this:

Come on then, you lot. Let's get this party on the road. This is the guard of the train I came down on. Black as the ace of spades and gorgeous. We're both as pissed as newts, so let's get this party swinging. Get the booze flowing and the bums writhing.

You must be Hilary. My God, little Miss Prim and Proper, eh? And this is Mr Wonderful, is it? Ye gods, did he fall or was he pushed? And you? Ye Gods, what a silly, boring suit. And what a silly boring man.

'There it is, daddy.'

'Oh God.'

'Doesn't it look cruel? Doesn't it look vicious with that yellow snout?'

'Yes.'

'I'm so nervous.'

'So am I. So am I.'

'Which side are we getting out from? I wish they'd tell you. The guard should announce it on his do-dah. It's very simple. Careful you don't take a rumble when he puts his brakes on. I think they do it deliberately, these drivers. They slam on their brakes so everyone lurches forward into each other, and they're sitting in the cabs laughing their heads off. It's the same with the guard. He's in his little hutch laughing his head off, because there's none of us know which side we're getting out of. I think it's disgusting. I'm going to complain.'

What if they're waiting for me at the barrier?
Oh God.
Surely not.
What will my entrance be then?
Oh God, I don't know.
Please, please, don't have them waiting at the barrier.
High speed train turn on your heel and whisk me back.
Please, please, please.

'Can you see her?'

'No.'

'Stand on your tippy toes.'

'I am.'

'Well?'

'No. I can't see her.'

'She's not come. I knew it. I knew she wouldn't come. I knew she'd funk out at the last minute. There was no reason for her to come. Thank God. Thank God. I'm glad she hasn't come. I'm glad . . .'

'There she is.'

'Where, where?'

'Now stick close to me, love. Look straight ahead and keep barging. When we get to the taxis, we'll push to the head of the queue and tell them it's an emergency. Well, if the Arabs can do it, so can we. It's our country, isn't it? I mean to say . . .'

'They're there.'

'What?'

'I can see them at the barrier. Oh, my God.'

'I see her.'

'Who's she with?'

'I don't know.'

'Wave to her.'

'She's stopped dead. She's turning back. She's running back to the train.'

Low key lady running back to high speed train.

Suburban parks.

Suburban gardens.

Sunshine of the country. Icy roar and snarl of tunnel.

Heron high above woods. Yackle of green woodpecker. Branch line curving through narrow cutting lined with rubble. A grey-bricked warehouse. A gap-roofed engine shed. An impatient level crossing.

Roar and rattle of slip stream. Blur of trees and fields and the spires of churches and the towers of timbered manor houses.

Lock gates.

A cottage.

A woman feeding the hens in the garden.

Black and white cattle.

Vomit in the toilet.

Dressed crab sandwiches.

A city of damp brown buses and sullen brick terraced houses.

Swans skidding squatly on ice-covered canal. Pied wagtails flickering and flittering on margins of sewerage farm. Tufted duck and pochard on thin-lipped reservoir.

Red anorak.

Snow-laden fields criss-crossed by the tracks of small and frightened animals.

Chill viaducts, soot-black brick lined cuttings, chattering points.

High speed train at rest in platform.

Low key lady stares at its snarling sneering front.

'You're so aggressive, high speed train. Fierce. Sneering. Snarling. So arrogant.

'You remind me of him.'

Low key lady in tight-belted burberry smiles her wistful smile once more.

She reaches out and strokes the snarling, sneering yellow snout of the high speed train.

'And you're handsome, too, high speed train,' she says. 'Yes, my dear. Yes, you *are* like him.'

The guard blows his whistle.

A porter shouts.

'Are you getting on this train, lady?'

She turns and smiles her wistful smile at him.

'No,' she says. 'Just watching.'

The high speed train pulls out, London-bound.

A tight-lipped lady stares out of her compartment window at the wistful lady with the long, elegant legs, standing on the platform, half waving, half smiling, her eyes filled with tears.

Chapter Seven

Silly woman.

I can't stand people who hang around on platforms like that.

They clutter up the place and make it look untidy.

Let's forget all about her, shall we?

A person who can afford a burberry like that, and spends her time slouching around railway stations is up to no good.

Am I right?

I am.

Good.

We've forgotten all about her.

Our main concern now is Mr Tattersall.

I call him Ernest.

You can, too, if you like.

I met him on one of my cruises.

He's a lovely little man, poor soul.

He looks after himself entirely on his own, and I must say he manages very well, considering.

That pot of home-made marmalade he sent me was delicious even though the skin was inclined to stick in your teeth if you ate it too quick.

He's got a lovely collection of George Formby records, too, and he keeps his lavvy absolutely spotless.

He's meeting me off the train, so we can spend Christmas together at our Hallam's.

Goodness knows what it'll be like.

This woman he's living with, Shirley, well, she's all right. In her way. But there's something about her I can't quite fathom out.

I mean, she must be peculiar, if she's willing to tolerate Hallam's poodle.

A poodle.

The mind boggles.

A grown man with a poodle.

I think it's unhealthy.

I do.

Mind you, I think there's a lot unhealthy about Hallam, and I'm his mother talking.

Before this Shirley, he never had a regular girl friend, you know.

I'm not implying that he's halfway to being a homo like that man in the paint shop with the hand-knitted ties and the funny thumbs, but I do think it's indicative.

He was always so secretive, when he was little.

He'd no time for his Meccano set, you know.

He was always up in his bedroom writing away in his red exercise books, and he'd never show you what he'd written.

When he was sixteen, I found one of his poems.

It was a love poem.

Disgusting.

It was all about pristine thighs and snow white orbs.

I didn't understand a word of it, and I knew instinctively it was rude.

Well, a mother has a second nature about these things, hasn't she?

It's the same way you know they're being disgusting in bed, when you see the state of the bottom of their vests.

Am I right?

I am.

Mm.

These dressed crab sandwiches are absolutely delicious.

They're scrumptious.

*   *   *

Three hours later the high speed train drew up in the main line terminal at London.

Mrs Place passed through the ticket barrier.

Standing there was a handsome middle-aged man in a smart suit. He held the hand of a blonde young lady.

She heard him say:

'She's not on it. I knew it. I knew it.'

She saw tears appear in the eyes of the girl, and then she saw Mr Tattersall waving to her.

'Ernest,' she said, and she shook his hand and he smiled and took hold of her suitcase.

'Now careful with that, Ernest. It's very heavy. We don't want you rupturing yourself. If you can't manage, we'll find a porter, even though they are all darkies.'

Mr Tattersall smiled again.

He picked up her suitcase and followed her as she barged her way through the crowds towards the taxi rank.

They waited for fifteen minutes, and then they installed themselves in a cab.

'There's just one thing, Ernest.'

'Yes, Nerys?'

'When we get there, don't make a fuss of Hallam's poodle.'

'Right, Nerys.'

'Leave it to me. I'll sort it out.'

'Right, Nerys.'

'A grown man with a poodle! Honest to God, Ernest, I swear I sometimes find it difficult to distinguish between them. I do.'

Well, that's me well and truly up the creek.

I've gone and crapped in their wardrobe.

Well, I was desperate.

He's been so busy getting things ready for his mother, he forgot to take me out on the common.

I was bursting.

I tried to tell him.

I kept giving him me paw and running to the back door, but all he did was give me a boot up the arse.

I tried her, too. Shirley. I gave her me paw and started panting, but all she did was shout for Hallam and tell him I was laddering her tights.

Women!

And listen – before we go any further, let's get one thing quite clear.

I am a standard poodle.

A big bugger.

I'm not like those poncey little toys and miniatures.

And I've not been clipped neither.

They've not got me cut like a raging pooftah with bobbles and flounces and a bare arse.

I'm all unkempt and untidy with apricot wool all over me eyes and me balls.

Right?

Good.

Hullo.

He's found out.

He's discovered the present I left for him in his wardrobe.

I think I'd better hide under the kitchen table.

'That's it then. That is it.'

Hallam Place, hair awry, trousers creased, stormed into the living room of his ground floor flat on Wimbledon Common.

'What is it?'

Shirley turned to him.

'The ultimate horror,' said Hallam Place. 'Wilfred has crapped in the wardrobe.'

'Don't be so ridiculous.'

'I'm not being ridiculous. It's true.'

'How can a dog crap in a wardrobe?'

'Very simple, my dear,' said Hallam Place. 'Someone leaves the wardrobe door open. The dog sees it. Whoopee, he says to himself. He gets inside, has a good sniff, has a good squat, and, hey presto, my brand new navy blue Kickers gone for a burton.'

Shirley threw back her head and began to laugh.

'It's no laughing matter, Shirley. That dog has got to go. I've given him his chances. He's had warnings. Last time he did it in the airing cupboard, I gave him the final ultimatum. Well, he's ignored it. So he goes to the vet right now. This very minute.'

'On Christmas Eve?'

'Yes.'

'Happy Christmas, Wilfred.'

Hallam Place buried his face in his hands and groaned.

'You don't take him out often enough,' said Shirley, resuming her decoration of the Christmas tree.

'What?'

'A quarter of an hour each day on the common is not long enough.'

'A quarter of an hour?' said Hallam Place. 'Do you know how long I was out with him this morning?'

'Tell me,' said Shirley, draping another strand of tinsel over the boughs of the tree.

'An hour. One full hour. And do you know what I was doing?'

'Tell me.'

'Waiting for him to perform. Prowling around after him. Watching his every move. Watching his every expression. Willing him on. Praying for him. Straining for him. But nothing. Not a thing. "Come on, Wilfred," I said. "You can do it. There's a good boy. You can do it, if you try." Nothing.

'I'm a ruined man, Shirley.

'The centre of my universe, the whole fulcrum of my being is centred on two square inches of a dog's arsehole.'

'How flattering for me.'

Hallam Place sank down on the sofa.

'I will take him to the vet, Shirley,' he said. 'One more time. Just one time. And it's curtains.'

'Good,' said Shirley. 'So we can let him out of the condemned cell, can we?'

Hallam Place paused. Then he smiled.

'Why not?'

Shirley put down the baubles, went over to the sofa and kissed Hallam Place full on the lips.

He grunted with pleasure and placed his hands on her breasts.

She paused for a moment and then she went to the door of the kitchen and called out:

'Wilfred. Good boy. Wilfred.'

Right then.

This is my cue.

Action stations.

Clear the decks.

Head hunched into shoulders.

Daft grin on my face.

And into the living room at a rate of knots and hurl myself on his lap.

'Wilfred, Wilfred, for Christ's sakes, get down.'

He doesn't mean it.

Nibble at his ear. Lick his face. Squat on his chest.

'Get off. For God's sake, get off.'

He's laughing really.

So's she.

Right, I'll give her the works now.

'Get down Wilfred. You're laddering my tights.'

All right, all right, I'll get down. I'll . . .

Oooh.

I've got this itch again in my do-dahs.

'Oh God, Shirley, he's sucking his nuts again. For God's sake, stop it.'

Hey up, there's no need for that.

I do object to getting a boot in my backside when I'm attending to a call of nature.

If only he'd shave some of the wool off my whatsits, I wouldn't have to nibble them like this.

Well, it's agony, I can tell you.

How would you like to have hairy balls in a centrally-heated flat?

It's agony, I tell you.

Hey up, there's a ring at the door.

It'll be his mother.

Oh God.

I'd better bark, I suppose.

What a drag.

It's bloody awful having a reputation as a good house dog.

Sometimes I wish I was a hamster.

Two hours later Mrs Place, Mr Tattersall, Hallam Place and Shirley sat in the living room, finishing off their afternoon tea.

They had had pikelets and scones and fancies.

Mrs Place had brought the pikelets from the north, and Mr Tattersall had bought the fancies from the shop on the corner of the street, where he lived.

Everyone was replete.

Mrs Place turned to Mr Tattersall.

'I wish you'd sit up in your chair, Ernest,' she said. 'I can't stand a man who slouches. It's right indicative, is that. Now then, Hallam, you were saying?'

'Was I?'

'Course you weren't. I was. I was telling you about the purser on our cruise. What was his name, Ernest?'

'I don't know,' said Mr Tattersall.

'You do.'

'I don't.'

'Now look here, Ernest, I'm not having argey bargey. I remember you writing his name down, don't I, Shirley?'

'I haven't the faintest idea,' said Shirley, stifling a yawn.

'Course you haven't. You weren't there, were you, love?' said Mrs Place, and she placed her hand on Shirley's knee and squeezed it. 'Well, any road, he was the most objectionable purser I have ever met in my life. And, let me tell you, I have met a good few objectionable pursers in my time. I'm that sort of woman.'

Mr Tattersall yawned.

And then he giggled when Mrs Place glared at him.

She continued with a sniff and a twitch of her shoulders.

'You see, it's not that I objected in principle to sharing a table with those Belgians. It's not that I've got anything against Belgians. It's just that I don't like them as a race. What was their name again, Ernest?'

'I don't know,' said Mr Tattersall.

'You do.'

'I don't.'

'Oooh, argey bargey again.

'Am I right?

'I am.

'Listen, you. Don't argue with me on questions of fact. I remember you writing their name down, don't I, Hallam?'

Hallam Place shifted in his seat.

'I haven't the faintest idea.'

'Course you haven't. You weren't there,' said Mrs Place. 'Anyway, she was quite nice in her own way, if you like that sort of thing. But him? He was a swine. He was a manufacturer of stapling machines and bulldog clips. Not that I hold that against him. But somehow it was right indicative, wasn't it?'

She was interrupted by her son.

'Where's Wilfred?' he said.

'He's under the table, isn't he?' said Shirley.

Hallam Place looked under the table.

'No, he's not there,' he said. And he called out: 'Wilfred. Wilfred, here, good boy.'

There was no response from the dog.

'He's not got out again, has he?' said Shirley.

Hallam Place groaned and jumped out of the sofa.

'Dear oh dear,' he said. 'What a Christmas. I'll go and look for him.'

He slouched out of the room, hands deep in his pockets, scowling.

Mrs Place twitched her shoulders and sniffed hard again.

'And as for the captain,' she said. 'Supercilious devil. I went up to him at his cocktail party, Shirley, and I said to him: "Look here. You might be good at driving your ship. But as far as providing decent cabaret's concerned, you're rubbish." You should have seen the look he gave. Just like the manager of the Co-op soft furnishing department when he . . .'

From the kitchen came a sudden howl of horror, of rage and of deep despair.

They turned to the door.

There was silence for a moment, and then Hallam appeared, holding an unseen object behind his back.

'That's it then,' he said.

'What?' said Shirley.

'The ultimate horror.'

'What for heaven's sake? What?' shouted Shirley.

Hallam showed the object he had been hiding behind his back.

'This,' he said. 'Wilfred's eaten half the goose.'

I'm in for it now.

Another kick up the backside.

Another screaming match.

Well, it's not my fault.

The silly sods never fed me.

In any case I'm a congenital thief. All standard poodles are. Did you know that? I bet you didn't.

I'd pinch anything.

As a matter of principle.

Pork pies, butter, eggs, stir 'n fry jock straps – it's all grist to the mill for me.

My policy is – nick now pay for it later.

And I'm certainly going to pay for this one.

Oh, by God, there's going to be all hell let loose.

That's why I've run away.

I'm on Wimbledon Common now. As soon as I'd nicked the goose, which, incidentally, tasted bloody awful, I crept out of the kitchen, crawled through the hole in the fence and pissed off quick to the common.

I hope you'll excuse the language. All that swearing. It's not very nice, I know. Particularly for a pedigree poodle. But bloody hell living with these two jerks would drive a bleeding saint to cursing. No wonder my language is so bloody diabolical.

What a couple of prize pillocks.

Do you know why they got me?

To stop them splitting up.

Honest. It's true.

Some people have a baby to try to keep their relationship in order.

They get a standard poodle.

See what I mean?

Pots for bloody rags.

What do you think to Phil Drabble on the telly?

Shit hot, eh?

I sometimes wish he'd get a new set of teeth, but . . .

Hello, there's that barmy red setter.

I'll just hide under this bench.
I can't stand the buggers.
Daft?
Bloody maniacs, man.
Charge all over the place, barking their heads off, running round in circles and making a thoroughgoing bloody nuisance of themselves.
You come on the common, and all you want are some interesting smells and a damn good shit, and these red setters come charging across to you, yapping and mithering the life out of you.
I'd ban them.
I'd . . .
He's gone.
What am I going to do now, though?
I daren't go home.
He'll kill me.
But it's getting cold here, and I think it's coming on to rain, too.
Oh hell, I wish I hadn't done it.

Mrs Place and Mr Tattersall were safely tucked up in their respective beds.

Shirley lay on the sofa in the living room, drinking a gin and tonic and smoking a fat Turkish cigarette.

Over her black nightgown she wore a flimsy lace black shawl.

Her plum red nipples glowed.

The front door slammed, and almost immediately Hallam Place entered the living room.

He was wearing a shabby RAF greatcoat, green wellington boots and a brilliant yellow sou'wester.

'Well?' said Shirley.

'Not a trace of him,' said Hallam Place. 'He must have got out through that hole in the fence.'

'Oh hell,' said Shirley. 'Do you want a drink?'

Hallam Place shook his head.

'I've been down as far as the Fox and Grapes,' he said. 'I've been halfway down the Ridgeway. I've been standing on street corners shouting and whistling and waving my arms and peering under hedges. I've been stopped by a police car.'

'Why?'

'Darling, it is ten minutes past midnight. It's Christmas morning.'

'Happy Christmas.'

They kissed.

'I love you,' said Shirley.

'Poor Wilfred,' said Hallam Place, pulling away from her embrace. 'I shouldn't have threatened him like that.'

'I said I love you.'

'He's probably wandering on the common now. Lost. Screaming in panic. Whining, snivelling, whimpering. Or having a monster crap.'

'Did you hear what I just said?'

'No. What did you just say?'

'I said I . . . oh never mind.'

Shirley downed her drink in a gulp and commenced to pour herself another one from the tray on the stand next to the Bang and Olufsen.

Hallam Place watched her silently.

Then he said softly:

'What did you say?'

'Never mind,' said Shirley, keeping her back to him.

'No,' said Hallam Place. 'If you start something, finish it off. That's one of your more irritating habits, Shirley. You say something. I don't quite hear it. I ask you to repeat it. You start off and then you shrug your shoulders and say: "Never mind." It's terrible, Shirley. So frustrating. Now, come on, tell me what you were just saying?'

'Never mind,' said Shirley sharply and she clinked the ice cubes in her glass.

'You see,' said Hallam Place. 'You see.'

He took off his greatcoat and flapped his sou'wester in the hearth, where a simulated log fire burned disinterestedly and scorched the dust.

Shirley returned to the sofa.

'What are we going to do about Wilfred then?' she said.

Hallam Place shrugged his shoulders.

'I suppose we'll just have to wait and see if he finds his own way back,' said Shirley.

'He's not intelligent enough for that,' said Hallam Place.

Shirley laughed.

'Poor Wilfred,' she said.

'In fact, basically, at heart and deep down, I think he's a screaming bloody idiot,' said Hallam Place.

'So do I,' said Shirley. 'I don't look on him as a dog. I think he's a skin with a man inside.'

'That's what I am.'

'What?'

'Never mind.'

'Now you're doing it.'

Hallam Place went to the drinks tray and poured himself a large whisky.

He looked down on Shirley as she lay back on the sofa, her whole body relaxed, her hair glowing. Her shoulders were smooth and her ankles were slim. Her thin silver anklet glowed in the light of the fire.

'What happens if he doesn't come back?' said Hallam Place. 'Do we split up?'

'Do you want to?'

'I don't know,' said Hallam Place. He sat down on the floor at the side of the sofa, and Shirley began to massage his shoulders. He grunted. 'Are you happy?'

'Are you?' said Shirley.

Hallam Place shook his head slowly.

'Who knows?' he said.

Shirley rumpled his hair, and then flicked the back of his right ear with her thumb and forefinger. He cried out with pain, but before he could turn to complain, Shirley had rumpled his hair again.

'Do you think your mother and Mr Tattersall are lovers?' she said.

'Who knows?'

'So why are they together?'

'Who cares?'

'I care,' said Shirley, and there was a hint of anger in her voice. 'I care about people. I care about their lives. I care about their predicament. I worry about them. I want to help them. That's why I work for this God-awful, sodding charity and earn a load of peanuts. I do it, because I care about people.'

She stopped.

She was breathing heavily, and her face was flushed.

Hallam Place sat silently at her feet and rummaged idly in his glass of whisky with his little finger.

'Don't people interest you, Hallam?'

'No.'

'But you're a writer. You should care about people.'

'Why? Do they care about me?'

'Very funny,' said Shirley and she shifted back on the sofa so that her body wouldn't touch his. She took a sip of her drink and turned back to him and stared at him intently. 'Hallam, when Mr Tattersall walked through that door there, what did you see?'

'I saw a tall skinny man with a dewdrop on the end of his nose.'

'And what did you think?'

Hallam Place scratched his head for a moment. Then he smiled broadly and said:

'I thought – ah, here comes a tall skinny man with a dewdrop on the end of his nose.'

'But didn't you want to know about his background?' she said fiercely. 'Didn't you want to know how he met your mother, if he's any family, if he's divorced, if he's widowed.'

'No.'

'So what about me? Don't you ever want to get inside me?'

He shrugged his shoulders.

She jumped off the sofa and squatted on her haunches in front of him, prodding him in the chest with her forefinger.

'You don't, do you? You don't care. I cry, so you comfort me. But why am I crying? You're not interested. I shout. I scream. I rant. I rave. You shrug your shoulders. You make a joke. You look chastened. But why do I shout and scream and rant and rave? You're not interested. Why am I so involved in my work? Why do I spend all the hours God sends organizing collections, planning campaigns, farting around with charity marches, charity parachute jumps, charity this, charity that?'

She prodded him so hard in his chest he fell back on to the sofa. She stood above him. She glared at him.

'Why?' she shouted. 'Why, why, why?'

Oh, bloody hell, they're having another row.

I can hear her screaming her head off.

'Why, why, why?'

Can you hear it?

Diabolical, isn't it?

Incidentally, I'm outside the french windows, and I'm soaked to the skin and frozen to death.

That's why I've come back.

Well, I'd sooner get a kick up the backside than spend all night on that bloody common.

My dears, I might be a dog, but I do appreciate the old home comforts.

Oh hell, he's at it now.

Bellowing at the top of his voice.

What a pair.

I suppose I'd better stop them.

That's what I'm here for. To keep them together.

I could jump up at the window, I suppose.

I could have a good howl.

No. Let's be more subtle.

I'll give a tentative scratch at the window frame. Make them think I feel guilty.

I feel like having a fuss made of me.

Okay, here goes.

'You don't care about me, you pig,' screamed Shirley at the top of her voice. 'You don't care about anybody except yourself.'

'Shush a minute,' said Hallam Place.

'What?' said Shirley.

'Shush,' snapped Hallam Place. 'Bloody shush.'

He padded softly to the french windows, drew back the curtains and looked outside.

'It's him. It's Wilfred,' he cried.

He opened the windows and a great bundle of apricot matted sodden wool hurled itself at him and sent him reeling backwards on the floor.

He fought the dog, but it was insistent.

It hunched itself into his chest, licking his face and nibbling his ears and thumping the inside of his thighs with its stubby tail.

Hallam Place heaved and wrenched and shoved it to one side.

Wilfred placed his tail between his legs and cowered.

'Look at him, Shirley,' said Hallam Place. 'He's absolutely soaked.'

'Yes,' said Shirley quietly.

'Poor old Wilfred. You're shivering, mate,' said Hallam

Place. 'You're frozen to the marrow, aren't you?'

Shirley said very quietly:

'I'll get a towel.'

And very quietly she repaired to the kitchen.

Hallam crouched by the side of the dog.

It rolled over on to its back and opened its hind legs.

'Baby Wilf,' said Hallam Place. 'Who was out on his own on the nasty big black common. Who's the naughty boy who . . . Why am I talking to you like this? You don't understand a single word.'

The dog wagged its tail tentatively.

'Don't wag your tail like that, mate. You don't understand a word I'm saying to you. What a companion, eh? Perfect.'

Shirley returned to the living room with a towel under her arm.

Hallam Place did not hear her or see her as she walked softly across the room and stood behind him as he talked to the dog.

'So what makes you tick, Wilfred? And do I care? You're shivering. I comfort you. But do I know why you're shivering?

'Course I bloody do, mate.

'One – you're shivering because you've been out on the common and you're soaked to the skin. And two – you're petrified I'm going to kick the living daylights out of you. Right? Right.

'You see, Wilfred, I care about you. I know about you. I know what makes you tick.'

'Here's the towel,' said Shirley quietly.

Hallam Place turned round, smiled and took the towel. He began to rub the dog vigorously.

'There, there, Wilfred,' he said. 'We'll soon get you dry. We'll soon get you warm.'

'I love you, Hallam,' said Shirley. 'I love you, darling.'

Hallam continued to rub the dog.

He did not turn round.

Chapter Eight

Well, it's Christmas Day morning, and we're opening our presents.

She didn't make us a bad breakfast, didn't Shirley, only I wish she hadn't used beef sausages.

I cannot stand beef sausages. I cannot abide them.

And she used tinned mushrooms, too.

Mind you, I think mushrooms are vastly over-rated.

So's tuna fish.

They say you can't tell the difference from salmon, but you can.

It's not a patch on salmon, isn't tuna fish.

It's the same as that Cleo Laines. She's not a patch on Dame Vera Lynn, and she's never off the telly these days with her frizzy hair and her cleavage.

Pooh!

That dog doesn't half pong.

He wants to get it clipped, does Hallam.

It's cruelty to keep it in that state.

She's right.

My nadgers are on fire with all this wool round them.

Hello, his mother's slipping me something under the table.

It's a sausage.

Beef.

I can't stand beef sausages.

Still, I better eat it.

In all this excitement of giving each other presents they'll probably forget to feed me again.

Presents!

What a drag.

Look at them.

Shirley's given him binoculars, and he's trying to pretend they're the best thing he's had since sliced bread.

'Binoculars. Terrific, Shirley. Look, mum. Binoculars.'

Gawd love us and save us.

What he needs is a pair of clippers to cut his hair with. Talk about me being woolly. He's like a bloody fuzzy wuzzy with that mop of his.

Struth, here's another sausage.

He'll kill her if he finds out she's feeding me at the table. He can't stand it. Neither can I if the truth be known. All you get usually is bits of gristle and the pink bits off Battenburg cake.

It's enough to . . .

Hello, hello, here we go again.

More presents.

Isn't Christmas a thoroughgoing balls ache, when you come to think about it?

'Come here, Ernest. You've got all your cardigan buttons done up daft.'

Obediently Mr Tattersall moved over to Mrs Place.

She adjusted the buttons on his cardigan, clucking with her tongue and shaking her head.

When she finished, she pushed him away.

'There now,' she said. 'You can see his new cardigan in its pristine state. What do you think to it, Shirley?'

'Lovely,' said Shirley. 'It's one of the nicest cardigans I've ever seen.'

'I knitted it for him on the cruise, didn't I, Ernest?' said Mrs Place. 'Well, you've got to do something on these cruises otherwise you'd go out of your mind.

'Am I right?

'I am.

'All that relentless enjoyment. I only go to find fault, you know.

'Right then, Hallam open the present I've brought for you.'

Hallam Place began to tear at the paper of the parcel his mother pushed in front of him.

Mrs Place sniffed hard and continued:

'If ever you want something to complain about, cross the Atlantic on the QE2. It's appalling, isn't it, Ernest? That decor! All those revolting colours. It's like travelling in a gigantic packet of winegums, isn't it, Ernest? And the food! Disgusting, isn't it, Ernest?'

Before Mr Tattersall could reply she rapped him sharply on the wrist with the back of her fork.

'Oh yes it is. Don't contradict. The first time I met you, you told me you sicked up three breakfasts and a cup of bouillon on the QE2.'

'I didn't,' said Mr Tattersall.

'I beg your pardon, Ernest, but you did. I've got a photographic memory for hearing things, and I distinctly remember you telling me.'

She dismissed him with a wave of her hand and turned to her son who was extracting a small green and white striped umbrella-like object from his parcel.

He held it up and smiled weakly.

'An umbrella,' he said. 'Just what I wanted.'

Mrs Place snatched it out of his hands.

'It's not an umbrella. It's a hat,' she said.

She opened it up and revealed a small white headband over which was spread a green and white mini parasol.

'Well, go on,' she said. 'Put it on.'

Hallam Place put it on his head and smiled sheepishly.

'Great,' he said. 'Doesn't it fit well?'

Shirley stifled a laugh.

'You can wear it when you take Wilfred walks on the common,' she said.

'Thank you very much,' said Hallam Place icily.

'We got it in Barbados, didn't we, Ernest?' said Mrs Place.

'No,' said Mr Tattersall. 'Trinidad.'

'All right. Have it your way – Trinidad,' said Mrs Place. 'Dear God, Shirley, men are buggers for geography, aren't they?'

'I suppose they are,' said Shirley, and then she lifted a corner of the tablecloth and said: 'Wilfred. Sit down. There's a good boy.'

'Bless him, isn't he obedient?' said Mrs Place. 'I don't suppose he's old enough to have started doing disgusting things with his do-dahs, is he, Shirley?'

She turned to Hallam once more and smiled.

'It suits you, does that,' she said. 'It'll come in right handy, won't it, Shirley?'

Shirley stifled another laugh.

'Oh yes,' she said. 'I've been trying to persuade him to get one for ages.'

'Well, you'll not get one in this country, Shirley, love,' said Mrs Place. 'They make them special in Barbados special for . . .'

'Trinidad,' said Mr Tattersall.

'All right, Ernest, all right. Trinidad,' said Mrs Place, and she flicked her shoulders. 'They make them in Trinidad special for the cricket. And when it comes on to rain, all the little nigger boys wear them. They do look lovely with their white teeth and their bloodshot eyes.'

Oh hell, he's started now.

Mr Tattersall.

He's slipped me a piece of toast.

I don't like toast.

It gets stuck in me teeth.

God, I could do with a crap.

He's not taken me on the common yet.

He's probably forgotten all about me.

Tell you what, if I give myself a good old scratch under the chin, he'll know I'm here and he might remember to take me out.

Here goes then.

'Wilfred,' shouted Shirley. 'Will you stop scratching yourself like that.'

'He's probably lousy with fleas,' said Mrs Place. 'What he needs is a damn good bath and a course of Bob Martins.

'Am I right?

'I am.'

Hallam Place hunched his head into his shoulders and scowled.

Mrs Place turned to Shirley.

'Now then, love,' she said. 'I don't want to badger you, but have you had any further thoughts regarding Christmas dinner?'

'Oh Lord, I forgot all about it,' said Shirley.

'Never mind,' said Mrs Place. 'Have you got a tin of ham in?'

'No.'

'You've not got a tin of ham in?'

'No.'

'Well, I never,' said Mrs Place. 'Fancy not having a tin of ham in. Isn't it unusual not having a tin of ham in, Ernest?'

Mr Tattersall shrugged his shoulders.

'Now don't look at me in that tone of voice, Ernest,' said Mrs Place. 'Ee, Shirley, aren't men argumentative? It's their hormones, you know. They've got far too many.'

The dog began to scratch itself again.

'Sit,' shouted Mrs Place, and the dog stopped scratching immediately. She smiled with pleasure and rested her hand on Shirley's forearm. 'Well then, love, if you've not got a tin of ham in, we'll have to put our thinking caps on, won't we?'

'We could always go down to the parade and see if that little Pakistani grocer is open.'

'Oh no, Shirley. Oh no,' said Mrs Place. 'I'm not going to no Pakistani grocer for my Christmas dinner. It's tantamount to blasphemy, is that. Our Lord'd do His nut, if He . . . Will you sit, Wilfred.'

'It's feeding him at the table that's doing it,' said Hallam Place. 'I told you not to do it.'

'You hold your hush,' said Mrs Place. Then she stood up and said: 'Right then, Shirley, leave it all to me. Let's get stuck into your pantry and see what you've got in.'

Shirley rose from the table with a sigh.

'Quite honestly I don't think there's much in,' she said.

'There's a few tins of Pedigree Chum, isn't there?' said Hallam Place, and Mr Tattersall tittered.

Mrs Place turned to her son and her lips curled back.

'Pay him no heed, Shirley,' she said. 'Let's go to the kitchen.'

The two women moved away from the table.

As soon as they did Wilfred shot out and bounded over towards them.

Hallam leapt off his chair and hauled him back by the collar, heaving and straining and panting.

His mother watched him silently for a moment, and then she said:

'It's a good job you never wanted to be in a circus, Hallam. You'd have been rubbish as an animal trainer. Rubbish.'

And then she left the room with Shirley.

Chapter Nine

They're still in the kitchen, are the two women.

I'm in the living room with him and Mr Tattersall.

And, I kid you not, my dears, I am in big trouble.

Well, he didn't take me out, did he?

And what happened?

You've guessed it.

A dollop of how's your father in the corner next to the hi-fi.

There's just one minor consolation, I suppose.

At least I missed his Barbara Dickson records.

They're drinking port and brandy.

They're not saying much, but they look pretty contented.

Well, wouldn't you be?

There's nothing worse than yacking women and . . .

Oh God.

He's spotted it.

'Oh my God.

'Who's done that?

'You bad dog.

'I'll bloody well murder you.'

The bugger!

He lashed out with his foot at me.

Good job, I'm light on me pins.

Well, all poodles are like that.

That's why they bung us in circuses and dress us up in frocks and make us look like thundering great eejits.

Bastards!

'For Pete's sake, Ernest. Don't tell the women. My mother will give me a sharacking as though I've done it myself. Now we've got to get it up before they come back.'

He's looking round helplessly.

He's scratching his head.

He always does at times of crisis.

What a useless berk.

'How am I going to scoop it up, Ernest?'

He's just as bad, Mr Tattersall.

He's not got a clue what to do.

It's obvious.

Scoop it up in your umbrella hat.

Ah.

He's cottoned on at long last.

He's taking his hat off, he's scooping it up in his hat and he's sticking it outside the french windows.

Good thinking, me old wingsy bash.

Go to the top of the class.

Hallam Place threw his umbrella hat behind the sofa and wagged his finger at Wilfred.

'One more time, mate. Just one more time. I'm warning you.'

Wilfred stretched himself out on the rug and rested his chin on his paws.

'Care for another drink, Ernest?'

Mr Tattersall nodded, and Hallam Place refilled their glasses with port and brandy.

Mr Tattersall took a sip and smacked his lips with pleasure.

He settled himself back in his chair and smiled at Hallam Place.

'So what do you do for a living?' he said.

Oh God, here we go again.

Spew it all out, Hallam.

That's it.

Get stuck into it.

Wrote a comedy series for telly.

Right?

Made a stick of money out of it.

Right?

Blew it all on buying this flat.

Right?

Haven't written a single thing since. Don't want to make people laugh. Why should I? They don't make me laugh.

Right?

People are loathsome. People are disgusting. People give me a right royal pain up the nose.

Right?

And what do I do now?

Now I sponge off my mother.

Right, Hallam?

Right, you boring, conceited, self-satisfied smug old wanker?

Churn it out.

Get it off your chest.

'No, I don't get bored, Ernest. Far from it. I find doing nothing is very stimulating. It keeps the mind occupied, Ernest. Keeps it fresh and lively. Keeps it pure. Keeps it innocent.'

His mother's voice called stridently from the kitchen.

'Ernest! Will you come in here a moment, Ernest.'

Mr Tattersall tittered and smiled weakly.

'Off you go, Ernest,' said Hallam Place. 'See you. Have fun.'

Mr Tattersall put down his drink on the low occasional table and with another damp smile left the living room for the kitchen.

Hallam Place clicked his fingers at the dog.

'Come here, Wilfred. Come on. I won't wallop you.'

The dog scuttered across the room on its belly and pressed itself into his legs, grunting with pleasure as he scratched its chin and its ears.

'There's the lad, Wilfred,' said Hallam Place. 'You know what I mean, don't you, Wilfred? There's nothing in the world like doing nothing. Perfection. Just perfection.'

He stood up.

'Come on. Let's go for a walk on the common. That's the next best thing to doing nothing.'

We're on the common now.

So are all the other silly buggers.

Look at that basset hound.

Who the hell ever thought of inventing a hound to hunt bassets?

Must have been off his beanpole.

And disobedient!

My dears, it doesn't know the meaning of obeying instructions.

The same as that long-haired dachshund.

The geezer who takes it a walk is reduced to tears sometimes.

Still, he'll probably prefer that to stopping at home with his missus.

You should see her.

All teeth and Jaeger jackets.

I bet she gives him a dog's life.

And what about that bloody stupid Pekinese that's always running round in circles yapping?

If I had my way, I'd . . .

'Fetch, Wilfred. Fetch. There's a good boy.'

Oh God, he's thrown a stick for me.

If there's one thing I detest more than anything else in the world it's chasing sticks.

What's the point in it?

Arseholes.

I'm stopping where I am.

'Fetch, Wilfred. Fetch.'

No.

'Ach. Why should you? I wouldn't.'

Course you wouldn't, you lazy berk.

'Do nothing, mate. Be like me.'

Exactly.

Good thinking, boy wonder.

'Basically, Wilfred, I think I'm more like you than I'm like me.

'You haven't got any good, decent, noble causes that are dear to your heart, have you?'

Not a single one, mate.

Though I wouldn't mind seeing a bit more of Phil Drabble and his sheep dogs on the telly.

Bloody marvellous, they are.

Well, it's their owners, you see.

They're not great lazy buggers like him who . . .

'You don't lie awake at night worrying about the Vietnamese boat people, do you, Wilfred?'

That I don't sunshine.

'I couldn't give a fart for the Vietnamese boat people.

'Starving millions in Bangladesh? Typhoon victims in the South Seas? Battered babies? The year of the disabled?

'I don't give a bugger.

'Wilfred, I am not interested.

'Wilfred, I am profoundly disinterested.

'I am not bothered.'

Yes, yes, yes, we've heard all that before.

Put a new needle in the gramophone record, eh?

'Do you know what bothers me, Wilfred?'

Haven't a clue, mate.

'I'll tell you.'

Oh hell, here we go again.

'I bother about that lime tree over there.

'Last summer it was a mass of yellow blossom. And it smelled something wonderful. I could smell it on my clothes for months after. I can still smell it now.

'And that's what bothers me now.

'Will it bloom again next summer?

'Will the swifts come again? And the swallows and the house martins? What's happened to the green woodpecker? Where are the pied wagtails and the wrens?'

Not bad.

I agree with you there.

'Bugger it, Wilfred. Don't fetch the stick. Sponge off us like I sponge off my mother. Let's go home. They'll have done the dinner with a bit of luck.

'With a bit of luck they might all have vanished.'

Chapter Ten

The Christmas dinner was over.

The revellers sat round the table in the living room replete and wearing funny hats of purple and pink.

The dog lay beneath the table.

Thin winter sunlight cast haggard shafts through the french windows. A herring gull yapped. A car door slammed.

The dog's stomach rumbled.

'Well, Shirley,' said Mrs Place. 'I say it myself, but that was a marvellous Christmas dinner.'

'Thank you,' said Shirley icily.

'No, fair's fair, love, you did do your bit,' said Mrs Place. 'But if it hadn't been for me making the corned beef hash, we'd have looked a bit silly, wouldn't we? You see, Shirley, with your larder being so badly stocked . . .'

'It's not badly stocked,' said Hallam Place.

'It is,' said Mrs Place. 'Compared to some.'

'Oh God, don't make matters worse,' said Hallam Place.

Mrs Place spun round in her chair to face him. Her eyes blazed.

'I am not making matters worse,' she said.

'You are.'

Mrs Place squared her chin and sniffed.

'I see,' she said. 'Thank you very much indeed.'

'Now don't get all hot and bothered,' said Hallam Place. 'It was bad enough last Christmas when . . .'

'What do you mean – it was bad enough last Christmas?'

'That fuss you made when Mr Pollard got the mince tart stuck under his dentures.'

Mrs Place's face broke into a warm smile.

'Mr Pollard! What a lovely man,' she said. 'He'd those lovely snow white dentures, had Mr Pollard. I met him on the Oriana.'

'The Canberra,' said Mr Tattersall.

'All right. Have it your own way, Ernest – the Canberra,' said Mrs Place. 'How do you know any road?'

'You've told me often enough.'

'I have not told you often enough, Ernest,' said Mrs Place. 'Are you implying that I've rammed it down your gullet?'

'No,' said Mr Tattersall.

'I should hope not indeed. I am not in the habit of ramming things down people's gullets.

'Am I right?

'I am.'

She glared at Mr Tattersall, who shrank back in his seat a little and tittered.

'If I've mentioned Mr Pollard once or twice, it's only because I was very fond of him,' said Mrs Place. 'He had a lot to recommend him, had Mr Pollard. He was an excellent sailor, and he was very good at quizzes, too.

'He wasn't very mobile, I grant you. But you don't expect to be jumping over five barred gates, when you've got an artificial hip joint, do you?

'I mean to say, he was always politeness personified to me. And he'd a lovely way with those Goanese waiters. He used to shout so they could understand his English.'

Look at them.

Listen to them.

What a family.

Trust me to get mixed up in a mad house like this.

Still, I reckon it'll all be over soon.

Well, him and Shirley can't last together much longer.

All those rows.

It's not her fault, mind you.

It's him.

He doesn't give a bugger about anything but me.

A poodle.

It doesn't make sense, does it? It's unhealthy. It's funny farm time, isn't it?

You know what?

When he talks to me, I think he's really talking to himself.

I do.

Honest.

Some of the things he tells me – they'd make your hair stand on end.

All those long involved stories about his marriage, his kids, his divorce, his affairs, his mistresses, his marriage again, his kids again – barmy.

He's never been married in his life.

I feel sorry for her.

Very nice, she is.

A good looker.

Kind, gentle, considerate.

And he treats her like shit.

Oooh.

Excuse me a minute.

Must have a good scratch and fleck.

That's better.

Where was I?

Ah yes, Hallam and Shirley.

I'll tell you the truth – I'm getting fed up with them.

I am. Honest.

I mean, it's such a responsibility. I'm supposed to be the one who's keeping them together. They've said it time and time again – it's only me that's keeping them together.

If I go, they split up.

Well, listen.

I've a good mind to bugger off here and now . . .

Struth, my skin's on fire.

My nose is warm, too.

Oh hell, I'm not sickening for something, am I?

Give myself another good scratch and fleck.

Ooogh.

Where was I?

Ah yes, I was talking about buggering off and leaving them.

Wouldn't you?

I mean, I make all this effort to be nice, to please them, to pander to their every whim, and still they're always having rows.

Do you know – I don't feel well at all.

I can't get comfy under the table.

If I sneak out very quietly like so and crawl on my belly like so and very quietly hoist myself on the sofa like so they won't spot me and I can have a good stretch in peace and comfort like so.

That's better.

Can't whack a bit of the old creature comforts, can you?

Do you know, I look at her sometimes, and I wonder to myself – does she really like me?

I don't think she does.

In fact, I'm convinced she hates my guts.

I think deep down and secretly she'd like me to go.

I think she's convinced that it's me that's causing all the rows between her and Hallam.

In fact, she's rumbled it.

She knows that it's all a load of old codswallop about me being the only thing that's keeping them together.

That's just Hallam's excuse for having me.

She'd never have worn buying a poodle in the first place if he hadn't weaved that yarn about it being the last chance to keep them together.

Bollocks.

It was just an excuse for him to own a poodle.

If I was her, I'd clear off and leave him and me together.

That's the only combination that stands a chance of success – him and me.

Her and him?

A non-starter, my dears.

No chance.

Ooooh. Struth.

I've just got to have another fleck.

I hope they don't notice.

If I sort of roll over on my side very carefully and bring up my back leg to my chin like so, they might not notice and . . .

'Wilfred, get off that sofa,' shouted Shirley.

The dog drew back its ears and slipped off the sofa, tail between its legs, belly low to the ground.

'And stop that scratching, too,' said Shirley. 'On and on and on. It's driving me mad.'

'You know why he's doing that,' said Mrs Place. 'I'll tell you. He wants clipping.'

'That is precisely what I keep telling Hallam,' said Shirley.

Hallam Place sighed.

'For the umpteenth time – he is not being clipped,' he said, and he intercepted a smile of approval from Mr Tattersall.

'That's just being stubborn,' said Shirley.

'No, it's not.'

'Yes, it is,' said Mrs Place. 'And it's cruel, too.'

'Cruel?'

'Yes, cruel. Look at the state of him. All that wool over his eyes. He can't see. No wonder he keeps running into trees.'

'That has got nothing to do with it,' said Hallam Place angrily. 'He keeps running into trees because he won't look where he's going.'

'How can he look where he's going when he can't see?'

* * *

You see, you see?

Row after row after row.

And I'm the cause of it.

All right, I can see both sides of the case.

I *do* keep running into trees, because I can't see where I'm going.

But he's right to stand firm against them clipping me to look like a great raging pooftah.

You've seen these big poodles cut like lions and God knows what with bloody great bobbles on their tails and bare bellies and pom poms on their heads.

It's sheer cruelty, is that.

We're hunting dogs.

We're water dogs.

That's why we've got webbed feet and woolly coats.

They've made us into a laughing stock.

You should see me swim.

Red hot, I am.

You should see me . . .

They're still at it.

Still rowing.

On and on and on.

'Now come on, stop it, you two,' said Mrs Place hitting the table with the palm of her hand. 'It's Christmas day. It's not the time for rows and argey bargeys.'

Hallam Place and Shirley stopped instantly.

They cast down their eyes.

Hallam Place tapped his foot and Shirley tugged at a stray lock of hair at the nape of her neck.

'I'll tell you one thing,' said Mrs Place, looking at them triumphantly. 'You wouldn't be having all these argey bargeys, if he'd shift himself, get off his backside and find himself a job.'

'Oh no,' said Hallam Place. 'Not that again?'

'Don't look at me in that tone of voice, Hallam,' said Mrs Place. 'It's high time this matter was discussed in public. Am I right? I am.'

'Oh please,' said Shirley. 'Not now.'

'I'm sorry, Shirley, but it has to be said. This situation has gone on far too long. And I intend to have my say here and now.'

'But it's Christmas day,' said Hallam Place.

'What's that got to do with it?'

'Christmas day isn't the time to be talking about things like that.'

'I thought you said you didn't care about Christmas.'

'I don't,' said Hallam Place. 'But millions do. What about your Vietnamese boat people? What about your starving tribesmen in the Sahara? What about your deprived blacks in Brixton? They care about Christmas. I don't want to spoil it for them.'

Shirley shook her head sadly.

'Hallam, you're being silly,' she said.

'It's the only way to cope.'

'It is not the only way to cope,' snapped his mother. 'The way for you to cope is to get yourself a job.'

'Why?'

'Because it is not healthy for a grown man of your age not to have a job.'

'Why?'

'Because you have to be productive.'

'Why?'

'Because you have to make a contribution to life.'

'Why?'

Shirley interrupted before Mrs Place could reply.

'Because you can't opt out of society, Hallam,' she said.

'I'm not opting out of society,' said Hallam Place.

'You are,' said Mrs Place.

'I'm very much a part of society.'

'You are. You are not,' said Shirley, and once more her

voice was spiked with anger and despair.

'Listen,' said Hallam Place. 'I'm vital to you lot. I am one of nature's drones. I am a natural. Society cannot do without me. Without me to scorn, where is self righteousness? Where is virtue?'

'Rubbish,' said Mrs Place.

Hallam Place smashed his fist down upon the table.

'It is not rubbish,' he shouted. 'It is not.'

He paused.

Then he said softly:

'I am a natural. Unsullied. Untainted. Innocent. I am as innocent as that dog lying under the table.'

He pointed dramatically at the dog, but then his arm drooped and he gasped.

'Wilfred? Wilfred, what's wrong with you?'

He fell to his knees and placed his arms round the dog's shoulders.

'He's shivering. Feel his nose. It's red hot. He's not well. He's ill.'

Mrs Place looked down on the dog.

'Yes, he doesn't look at all good to me. He looks just like our Buster did before he conked out on us last Whitsuntide.'

Hallam buried his head into Wilfred's flank.

'Wilfred, what's the matter with you, my son? Wilfred, for Christ's sake, don't go on and conk out on us.'

Don't worry.

It's all a cod.

I'm not really poorly.

I just put it on to get him out of an awkward situation.

If I can swing this little pretence all over Christmas he might avoid getting bollocked by his mother.

And if he avoids that, he'll avoid having a real humdinger of a row with Shirley about them getting married and him going out to work or starting writing again and all that load of codswallops.

All I've got to do is keep this up for a couple of days, and he should be all right.

What a life, eh?

He's down there talking to the dog.

I know it's at death's door, but it's only an animal. And after all it is human nature for animals to die, isn't it?

Am I right?

I am.

I think his preoccupation with that dog is unhealthy.

I do.

I know it sounds funny, but sometimes I find it hard to distinguish between the two of them.

They're both bone idle. They're always bumping into things and tripping over their own big feet.

And they're not all they should be in matters regarding personal hygiene and ablutions activities.

I think there's something radically wrong with Hallam.

He's much worse since the last time I visited him.

I thought living with Shirley would sort of sort him out, but it hasn't.

All he seems to be doing these days is having argey bargey.

I mean, basically I don't approve of people living together when they're not married. I don't think it's conducive. However, in this case I was prepared to bend the rules and give it my approval because I thought Shirley would bring him to his senses.

It hasn't.

The only thing that's changed since I last saw him is that he's got even more obsessed with that poodle.

A poodle!

Madness.

All he does with himself is talk all night long with a poodle.

* * *

'God, Wilfred, don't conk out on us. Not on Christmas day, mate.

'Bloody Christmas.

'I detest it. Always have done. Too many people about. That's the whole trouble with me, Wilfred – there are too many people about in my life.

'It was bliss when I lived in this flat on my own. Wonderful. Lying in bed till two in the afternoon. Not washing the pots for a week. Doing what I didn't ought to in the sink.

'Marvellous.

'And then after a while people started to move into the flat. Mates I could have a good time with. Mates I could talk to. Frank Sinatra. Now he was a good mate. Rocky Marciano. So was he. Kim Novak. Wow! George Formby. Ramsbottom and Enoch. Collinson and Breen. Princess Margaret. Nice folk, Wilfred. Didn't impose. Buggered off home as soon as I asked them.

'But nice to talk to. Endlessly. Hour after hour after hour. I was never lonely.

'Sometimes we'd all go on the common and we'd meet up with other mates there. Johnny Carey, Cyril Washbrook, Albert Stubbins, Reg Harris, Arie Van Vliet, Fausto Coppi, Louison Bobet.

'We'd all go into the Fox and Grapes – in the side bar where it's all cool and dark. I'd buy a pint of John Courage. And I'd sit there, and I'd listen to my mates talking.

'And then there was the bliss of walking home to the flat, knowing that it would be absolutely, totally, completely deserted.

'Not a soul there.

'Not a trace of another human being.

'I was entirely self-contained, so self-sufficient, I feasted off myself. I could have eaten myself alive, picked the bones white, sucked the sinews, let the blood run down my chin.

'That was real life, Wilfred.

'That was reality.'

Chapter Eleven

It was the morning of Boxing Day.

Hallam Place lay fast asleep on the sofa in the living room.

The dog was curled up in its basket.

Mrs Place entered the room and pointed to it.

'Well?' she said. 'How is it?'

Shirley shrugged her shoulders.

'Not too good.'

'Bless him,' said Mrs Place. 'That's the trouble with dogs, isn't it? You get so attached to them. You treat them as one of the family. And then, when you least expect it, the ungrateful devils go and die on you.'

'He's not going to die,' said Shirley. 'He's just got a chill.'

'Maybe,' said Mrs Place. 'But if he should go and die, don't get another one. They're so tying, are dogs. Every time you go away you've got the nightmare of kennels . . .'

Suddenly she saw her son on the sofa.

'What's he doing here?'

'He stayed up all night with Wilfred. He's just conked out. He's absolutely exhausted.'

Mrs Place looked down on her son as he lay on the sofa, mouth open, arms twitching, moaning softly in his sleep.

'He doesn't look all that healthy to me,' she said. 'What does he do with himself all day long while you're out at work?'

'Goes out on the common,' said Shirley.

'And then?'

'Goes out on the common again.'

Mrs Place flicked her shoulders and tightened her lips.

'He watches too much television. Am I right? I am. He's

got the exact look of someone who watches telly during the day – brow-beaten, defeated.'

'He hates television,' said Shirley, and she emptied the contents of an ash tray into the wicker waste paper basket she carried under her arm.

She had her blonde hair tied at the nape of her neck with an elastic band.

Her arms were bare.

Mrs Place sat down on a dining chair and rested her elbows on the table thoughtfully.

'You know what he loved doing when he was little?' she said.

'What?' said Shirley, and she picked up one of Hallam's discarded socks and dropped it into the waste paper basket.

'Cycling. He was a bugger for cycling, was Hallam,' said Mrs Place. 'His father and me used to take him out every night on our bikes. We had matching Rudges. He always used to lag behind us, did Hallam. I used to think he was afraid of being seen with his dad's skinny ankles, but it wasn't that at all. He used to lag behind us so he could talk to himself. His father wanted to take him to the doctor. "I think we should take him to the doctor, Nerys," he said. "No, Edgar, no," I said. "It's just one of those passing phases," I said. Does he ever talk to himself now?'

Shirley spun round to face the sofa.

She opened her legs and placed her hands on her hips.

A slow smile came to her face. Slowly she walked to the sofa. Slowly she knelt down. Slowly she began to stroke Hallam Place's hair.

'Do you ever talk to yourself, Hallam?' she said. 'When I am not here, do you talk to yourself, my love?'

Silence.

Hallam Place grunted.

Suddenly Shirley prodded him hard on the shoulders with her right forefinger.

'Bastard,' she said. 'You bastard. Self-indulgent. Conceited.'

Hallam Place grunted again.

It was a grunt of contentment.

Shirley prodded him even more fiercely.

Her blonde hair came loose from the elastic band, and it glowed as it tumbled about her shoulders.

'I could run a toasting fork right through you, and you wouldn't move,' she said. 'I could twist your fingers right back to your wrists. I could put my two thumbs deep in your nostrils and wrench them apart. And you wouldn't move.

'No feeling. No response. Nothing. Bastard.'

Wilfred lowered his head deep into the depths of his basket. He began to shiver.

Shirley smiled to herself.

She rested her head on Hallam Place's chest and said softly:

'Hallam, my love. We were going to get married, weren't we? We'd planned it all out, hadn't we?'

Suddenly the tone of her voice changed.

The softness was replaced by a bleak harshness.

'As soon as my divorce came through we were going to get married, weren't we, my precious, loving, caring, darling?'

Mrs Place removed her elbows from the table. She sat upright in her chair, her body tense, her eyes narrowed.

Shirley softened her voice once more and began to stroke Hallam Place's thighs tenderly.

'My divorce came through,' she said. 'But you did nothing. I waited and waited. You said nothing. Not a single word. Not a bloody word.'

Suddenly she leaned forward and bellowed into his ear:

'What's going on in there? What's going on in that great hollow cave?'

Hallam Place hardly stirred.

'I'd come home from work, and you'd smile, and the flat

was not neat and tidy, it was as though you hadn't been living in it all day. I'd go out to the shops and buy things and cook a meal, and you'd eat it as though I wasn't there as though you were eating make-believe food.

'And at night, when we screwed it was as though you were making love to a make-believe woman.'

She paused.

The dog drew himself even deeper into the recesses of his basket.

'Is that what you want, Hallam?' said Shirley. 'A make-believe woman in a make-believe life?'

She's right.

She's hit the nail right on the head.

The only thing is, my dears, he's already living in his make-believe life.

The only thing that exists for him is me.

Shirley, his mother, Mr Tattersall, the man in the paper shop, the guy with the basset hound on the common – he looks on them as mere figments of his imagination.

It's true.

The only real thing in his life is me.

Poor sod.

Chapter Twelve

Breakfast was eaten in silence.

Shirley hardly raised her eyes from her plate. Hallam Place toyed with his food, limp-wristed and bored. Mr Tattersall ate heartily. Mrs Place stared long and hard at her son.

Finally she said:

'Well, I don't approve, Hallam.'

'Sorry?' said Hallam Place.

'I think it's disgraceful.'

'What?'

'I don't want to be brutal. I don't want to be cruel. But if you don't take a grip on yourself, young man, and make some drastic changes in your life, then this will be the last time I shall ever come to your flat at Christmas.'

Mr Tattersall commenced to wipe the grease off his plate with a wadge of white bread.

Shirley raised her eyes slowly to look at Hallam.

Wilfred shifted his position in his basket and yawned softly to himself.

Hallam Place dropped his fork on to his plate.

'What the hell are you talking about?' he said to his mother.

'I'm talking about your marriage,' she said.

'What marriage? What's she talking about, Shirley?'

'You know,' said Shirley very quietly.

'I don't,' said Hallam Place. 'What are you talking about?'

Mrs Place took a compact out of her handbag and began to powder her nose, looking at Hallam over the top of the mirror as she talked.

'I never realized for a moment you intended to get married,' she said. 'I wasn't aware of it till Shirley just told me while you were snoring your head off on the sofa.'

'Ah. Now I see.'

'Well, let me tell you here and now, I'm absolutely delighted. I'm over the moon, literally.'

'Christ.'

Mrs Place snapped her compact shut.

'There's no need to bring Him into it,' she said. 'You've got enough on your hands dealing with me. And I'm not going to pull any punches, me lad. I'm giving you a choice. Either you marry this girl and settle down with a substantial mortgage and decent bed linen, or I shall wash my hands of you completely and walk right out of your life. For ever.'

Hallam Place groaned.

He stood up and slouched to the french windows. He looked out silently for a moment and then he turned.

'I don't believe this,' he said. 'I don't believe this is happening. Boxing Day. The dog lying at death's door in the basket. And my mother's trying to marry us off. Is this really happening to us, Shirley?'

'Yes, it is,' said Shirley slowly and firmly.

'And there's something else about to happen,' said Mrs Place.

'What?' said her son.

'I'm cutting you off.'

Hallam Place giggled softly.

'Shirley?' he said. 'What's she talking about, Shirley?'

'Never mind Shirley,' said Mrs Place. 'You pay attention to me. I'm giving you an ultimatum. You sit down at that typewriter and start writing again, or I cut you off completely. There'll be no more money. No paying your bills. No helping you out of jams. You'll be entirely on your own.'

'I see.'

'No, you don't see. That's the whole point. Good heavens above, lad, there's people who'd give their hind teeth for a talent like yours.

'That comedy series of yours was the funniest thing I've seen for years. Mrs Cranston from the dry cleaners said it had her in pleats. The boss-eyed man who delivers the coal never stopped raving about it.

'And what have you done since?

'Nothing.

'You've the precious talent of being able to make people laugh and you've just frittered it away in bone idleness and talking to that poodle. Why? Why won't you use your talents?'

Hallam Place shook his head.

'Shirley,' he said. 'Shirley, help me.'

'Leave Shirley out of it,' snapped Mrs Place. 'It's your decision now. The ball's in your court. You have to do something positive. You have to marry this girl. You have to get down to your writing again. And unless you do that, I wash my hands of you completely and utterly. Well? What are you going to do?'

Hallam Place stood stock still.

He looked from face to face.

No one spoke. No one moved.

A chill smile came to his features, and he said:

'I'll tell you what I'm going to do. I'm going to get Wilfred another blanket.'

Shirley sprang up, knocking her chair to the floor.

'You bastard. You swine,' she screamed. 'Wilfred? I hate him. I loathe him. I despise him. I hope he dies. I hope he dies in agony. I hope he dies here and now in front of your very eyes.'

That's torn it.

They're going to split up.

No doubt about it.

I've failed.

I've made a right cods wallops of it, haven't I?

What should I do?

Shall I jump out of my basket and run round the room like a madman?

Shall I leap all over the furniture and grin at them like a gibbering idiot?

Shall I throw myself at their chests and lick their ears and nibble their necks?

It's too late for that.

Shirley's in the kitchen with his mother.

I can hear them jabbering.

Mr Tattersall?

I don't know.

Does he really exist?

Is he just a poodle like me for Hallam's mother?

Who cares?

I don't.

I don't give a shite.

What worries me is him.

He's kneeling in front of me as I lie in the basket.

He's talking to me.

'A great day, Wilfred.

'A perfect day.

'Happy Christmas one and all.

'Can you hear me, everyone?

'Good.

'Well listen.

'This day is perfect. There is nothing I like better than to be surrounded by people who give me love and affection, who care about my well-being, who worry about my future, who give me advice and solace, who fill my life with their compassion and their concern, who fill in the great emptiness and loneliness of my existence with the warmth and the strength and the vigour of their voices.

'Can you hear me, everyone?

'It's your voices I like.

'It's your voices and nothing else.'

In the kitchen Shirley looked at Mrs Place.

'You see,' she said. 'It can't go on.'

'No,' said Mrs Place.

'I can't live like this.'

'I know, love.'

'It's madness.'

'Course it is.'

'That dog. That bloody dog.'

I better do something.

Quick.

I know.

I'll pretend I'm better.

'Are you trying to wag your tail, Wilfred?

'You are.

'Are you feeling better?

'You are.

'Is Wilfred feeling better?

'Your nose isn't as hot as it was. And you're trying to lift your head. There, there. Who's a good boy? Who loves you?

'I do, Wilfred.

'I love you.'

'So now you see for yourself,' said Shirley to Mrs Place. 'That's the only thing that's real for him. Wilfred. A dog. Can you believe it? Can you understand it? Is it possible? Or am I just making it all up?'

*   *   *

I've done it.
He's swallowed it hook line and sinker.

'You've done it, Wilfred.
'You're on your feet.
'Shirley.
'Shirley, Shirley.
'Come here quickly.'

'Do I exist, Mrs Place?
'Is he aware of me?
'No.
'No, he's not. It's the dog. In the whole of his life the one reality is that dog.
'Wilfred. Bloody Wilfred.'

Well, I'm on my feet now.
Mustn't over-do it, mind.
Got to keep up the pretence.
I know.
I'll have a good yawn.
Dogs always yawn when they're embarrassed.
Have you noticed?
Oh God, he's bellowing for her again.
Here she comes.
This is it.

Shirley entered the living room.
She saw Hallam kneeling in front of the dog.
The dog was wagging its tail and yawning.
She spoke.
'What do you want?'
Hallam Place turned to her with a broad smile on his face.
'I wanted you to see Wilfred,' he said. 'He's better. Look

at him, Shirley. He's wagging his tail. He's . . . You're not interested, are you?'

'No, I am not interested,' said Shirley. 'In fact, I am profoundly disinterested.'

'I see,' said Hallam Place, and he turned away from her.

Shirley paused for a moment.

She looked round the room.

The sofa was rumpled. The dining table was neat. The dog wagged its tail nervously and tentatively and panted.

'I want to tell you something,' she said.

'Yes?'

'I'm leaving you.'

'I see,' said Hallam Place and very slowly he began to stroke Wilfred.

'Don't do that,' said Shirley, but he ignored her.

'When are you leaving?' he said.

'Today.'

'I see.'

'"I see, I see?" Is that all you can say?'

Hallam Place stood up slowly.

'I don't know what to say, Shirley. I don't know what to do,' he said.

She looked at him silently, and her eyes softened, and she moved forward a pace towards him.

'It's so difficult,' he said.

'I know,' she said, and her voice was gentle.

'Shirley,' he said, and he moved towards her.

'Yes?' she said, and her lips were moist.

'What I want to say, Shirley, is that I . . . Wilfred! Oh God, man, you've gone and crapped on the carpet.'

I couldn't help it.

Honest, I could not.

The daft bugger forgot to take me out again.

What could I do?

I'm a dead loss, me.
She's in the bedroom packing.
He's in the kitchen thrashing about.
And me?
Total and utter disgrace, my dears.
Talk about the dog house.
If looks could kill, I'd be . . .
Oh heck.
It's him.
Hallam.
He's come into the room.
Right then, Wilfred, my old sunshine, prepare for doom.

Very slowly Hallam entered the living room.

The dog crouched down on its belly and pumped its tail.

It cringed as Hallam Place kneeled down beside it.

It rolled over on to its back and hunched its woolly head into its woolly shoulders.

Hallam Place spoke softly to it.

'So that's it,' he said.

He shook his head.

'On our own, eh? Thee and me, Wilfred.'

He patted the dog's head slowly.

And then he smiled.

'I couldn't care less, old son. Honest. I don't feel pain. I don't feel relief. I feel nothing. Nichts. Grr nichts.'

He laughed.

'Frank Sinatra! Kim Novak! Johnny Carey! You can come out, lads. Come on then. Let's be having you.'

He laughed again.

Louder and louder and louder grew his laughter.

He's pots for rags, he is.
Totally off his bean pole.
Give over, will you.

He's starting to kiss me.
I can't stand people who kiss dogs.
It's so bloody unhygienic.
And I can't stand the smell of their breath neither.
All that . . .
Oh hell.
She's come in.
She's standing inside the door staring at him.
She's all dressed up and ready to leave.
I tell you what – she's a real cracker on the quiet.
She's subtle.
Know what I mean?
She's sort of soft and yielding and blurred at the edges.
Know what I mean?
She's the girl of your dreams.

Shirley walked across the room.

She bent down and kissed Hallam Place on the back of the neck.

'Look at him,' he said, pointing to the dog.

'Guilty. Cringing. He knows he's failed. He's still here and you're going.'

'That's right,' said Shirley.

'I hope you'll be happy.'

'And I hope you will.'

He stood up and kissed her lightly on the cheek.

She did not move.

'I'm sorry it didn't work out,' he said. 'I know it could have. If I'd been this. If I'd been that. But I couldn't change. I'm as I am, Shirley. Self-sufficient. Self-destructive. Self, self, self.'

She nodded.

And then she began to walk towards the door.

Hallam Place lowered his eyes.

And then just as she was about to leave the room and leave

the flat and leave him for good and all, a curious thing happened.

The dog sprang to its feet and barred her way out of the door.

'Wilfred,' she said. 'What do you want?'

The dog wagged its tail and gave her his paw, and stared into her eyes fiercely and intently.

'Do you, Wilfred? Do you?' she said.

The dog wagged its tail more furiously.

'Are you sure?'

The dog stood on its hind legs, and resting its paws on her shoulders, began to lick her face.

'You want to come with me, do you?'

The dog jumped up and down and wagged its tail hysterically.

Shirley paused.

She smiled.

'Okay,' she said. 'Come on then.'

Wilfred trotted out with her happily.

Well, what would you have done?

Think about it.

You just think about it deeply, my dears.

Chapter Thirteen

That's why I decided to take Hallam back home with me.

He didn't object.

He'd had all the stuffing knocked out of him.

Mr Tattersall took us to lunch at a very nice restaurant although the cabbage was overdone and the custard was stone cold, and then we took the train home.

I put him straight to bed.

He slept, and he slept, and he slept.

And eat?

When he was awake, he ate me out of house and home.

Liver and bacon and sprout tops. Shepherd's pie. Lancashire hot pot with mashed swede. Ox tail casserole. Cow heel stew. Tripe and onions. Belly pork done in the oven with oodles and oodles of crackling. Stuffed roast hearts with broad beans and parsley sauce. Meat and potato pie with carrots and turnips. Steak and kidney pudding with creamed spinach. Potted meat sandwiches. Pikelets. Polony. Haslet. Pigs' trotters.

You name it, he ate it.

But most of all he slept.

That's what he's doing now.

I've left him at home in bed while me and his brother, Garfield, drive over to see my Auntie Medora.

Chapter Fourteen

Garfield and his mother, Mrs Place, drove over the high moors.

Snow lay thickly on the rough pastures and was banked in deep ice blue drifts against the dry stone walls.

The roads were clear.

The sun shone.

Smoke from lazy village chimneys stood upright in the stinging blue sky.

In the nestling valleys the mills were chilled and silent.

On the bleak bogs and stark crags the winter wind hissed with frost.

You can't beat Northern scenery.

Am I right?

I am.

I mean, the scenery in the South can be very nice.

In its own way, of course.

But if you want scenery you can get your teeth into, give me the North any day of the week.

He's a very good driver, is Garfield.

Sensible and cautious.

He's as different from his brother, Hallam, as chalk is from cheese.

He is.

He's solid, upright, respectable and hard-working, is Garfield.

He's a lovely wife with immaculate taste in kitchen furniture.

He's a secure job as a junior executive in a shirt

manufacturing company with car provided and generous sickness and pension allowances.

He's a beautiful house with integral waste disposal and through lounge/diner.

And well deserves it.

Am I right?

I am.

You see, he wasn't like Hallam when he was little, wasn't Garfield.

He buckled down, did Garfield.

That's the only way to make a success out of life – buckle down and never park on a double yellow line.

I wish Hallam had followed those precepts.

Mind you, it could be hereditary, I suppose.

I mean, look at Aunt Medora.

Pots for rags, she was, last time I saw her which is some considerable time, I can tell you.

She always had this funny look in her eyes as though she was staring straight through you, yet mocking you, and she always seemed that she wasn't listening to you yet she found what you were saying was amusing.

I was terrified of her when I was little.

I once saw her running nude through her back garden.

I once . . .

There's only one thing I've got against Garfield – he will persist in playing his car radio too loud.

He's at it now.

Radio Two at full blast.

And what sticks in my gullet is that it's another one of those darkies singing.

They're never off the wireless these days.

Whoever told them they could sing wants his bumps feeling.

All they do is sing the same five words over and over again with no tune and a voice like an eel being skinned alive.

Am.I right?
I am.
What's wrong with our own, I say?
I don't think music's ever been the same since George Melachrino passed on.
And there's another thing I can't stand.
You're listening to the wireless happily, and then they break in and tell you they're changing over to Schools Broadcasts or the Open University.
So you've got to switch to another waveband then, haven't you?
What a performance.
Can you find the station you want all these killer hertzers and things on the dial.
What's wrong with having names?
What's happened to Hilversum and Droitwich and . . .
Oooh, I could go on.
I could.
I won't, though.
I'm going to sit back and enjoy the trip.
Mind you, if Mary O'Hara comes on the wireless . . .
I will.
Honestly, I will.

Auntie Medora lived in a substantial stone-built terrace house.
It had a steep front garden which sloped down to the street.
It was bare and haggard, for the soil was poor, and the winter frosts had cut back the shrubs and bushes.
A laurel drooped in a soot-stained terracotta pot.
The back garden was different.
It was lush and rampant.
There was a damp lawn straggled by borders of escallonia, skimmia, veronica, cypress and weeping cotoneaster.

There was an arbour entangled with Bourbon, musk and china roses.

There was a brooding high hedge of holly, ivy and berberis.

Auntie Medora stood at the french windows of her drawing room looking out over it.

She was extremely old.

She smiled at a blackbird which stood on the lawn, head on one side, peering intently at a minute patch of stubbled grass.

She turned and walked to the large marble fireplace.

She stared at herself in the mirror on the mantelpiece.

'I'm so ugly,' she said.

'I'm really, really ugly.

'I'm the ugliest woman in the whole world.'

She looked at her reflection intently, and when she smiled, it was as though she were looking straight through it at an image long distant.

She began to walk round the room slowly.

'I can see him,' she said.

'I can hear him.

'I can smell him and I can touch him and I can feel his breath.

'And he's dead.'

She laughed and returned to the mirror on the mantelpiece.

She examined her face from every angle.

'When I was young, I was so beautiful,' she said.

'Everyone said so. Jake said it. Thurston said it. "Medora," they said. "You're a real beauty," they said.

'And now look at me. I'm going bald. My hair's as dry as bracken. And look at my neck. It's a turkey's neck. I've got a moustache. I've a stubble on my chin. My skin's wrinkled and blotched.

'I'm really, really, really, really ugly.'

* * *

Half an hour later she answered a knock at her front door and admitted to her house Mrs Place and Garfield.

'Auntie Medora, how lovely to see you after all this time,' said Mrs Place. 'My word, you are looking well. Absolutely tip top. That's what comes of keeping your bowels regular. They were talking about bowels on the Jimmy Young show yesterday: Auntie Medora. Personally I think he's a detestable individual, but he does know his P's and Q's as regards laxatives.

'Am I right?

'I am.'

Auntie Medora smiled.

She took her niece by the arm and led her by the arm into her drawing room.

Garfield followed and stood in the doorway, fiddling with his cufflinks.

Auntie Medora spun round to face him and said:

'And who are you?'

'It's Garfield, Auntie Medora,' said Mrs Place. 'Last time you saw him he was only a baby. Well, he's grown up now. He's thirty eight and a half and he's a junior executive with a shirt manufacturing company. He's wearing one of their products now, aren't you, Garfield?'

'Yes,' said Garfield.

Auntie Medora smiled her smile at him, and he smiled back.

'Garfield!' said Mrs Place. 'Don't stare at your Auntie Medora like that. It's very rude to stare at people, isn't it, Auntie Medora?'

'I don't mind,' said Auntie Medora. 'I like being stared at. I was so beautiful.'

She ran her fingers down her neck.

She did it very slowly.

'Come here, Garfield,' she said.

Garfield coughed nervously.

'Come on,' she said. 'I won't hurt you.'

He walked towards her.

She smiled at him once more and began to rub his cheeks.

'There, Garfield,' she said. 'There, there.'

Suddenly an insistent, high-pitched buzzing noise wriggled into the room and cackled.

'What on earth's that?' said Mrs Place.

'It's my computer buzzer,' said Garfield.

'That again,' said Mrs Place. 'It's the bane of my life, is that computer buzzer. Why he's got to have one I just do not know.'

'I've told you, mother,' said Garfield. 'It's for my work.'

'Rubbish,' said Mrs Place. 'Your Uncle Hitchcock never had one. And look how high he rose in the gas showrooms.'

Garfield sighed deeply.

'I need it to keep in touch with the office,' he said.

'Not when you're at the Christmas panto you don't,' said Mrs Place. 'Honestly, Auntie Medora, we all went to the Christmas Panto at the Grand last Christmas and halfway through Clodagh Rodgers – if you like that sort of thing – his little computer buzzer went off. I just did not know where to put myself, and you could see Nat Jackley as Baron Hardup noticed it, too.'

Why wasn't I like Hallam?

Why did I always buckle down and take the easy way out and . . .

No, it wasn't the easy way out.

I liked being ordinary.

I liked being mediocre and conventional and having integral waste disposal and a through lounge/diner and a garden full of suburban roses.

But it would have been nice to have been like Hallam.

All those women he must have in London.

All those famous people he must meet.

I wonder if he knows David Vine?

I wonder if he . . .

I like working for a shirt manufacturing company.

I do.

Course I do.

Course I bloody do.

Auntie Medora smiled once more at Garfield.

It made him feel warm and secure.

'Would you like to telephone your office, Garfield?' she said.

'Well, yes, as a matter of fact, I would,' he said.

'Then make your telephone call, Garfield,' said Auntie Medora.

'Thank you,' said Garfield.

He paused.

For the first time he noticed that every item of furniture in the drawing room was covered in heavy linen dust sheets.

Why?

Why am I so unobservant?

When we were brothers together at home Hallam noticed everything.

Ships' funnels, birds' plumage, locomotives' numbers, names written on the side of railway freight waggons.

I never noticed that railway freight waggons had names like Seacow and Sealion and Narwhale.

If I'd noticed that, my life would have been so much more rewarding.

'Sit there while you make your phone call, Garfield,' said Auntie Medora.

She pointed to a dust sheet-covered armchair.

Garfield paused, for underneath the sheets was a curious shape.

Auntie Medora pulled back the covers to reveal a stuffed dog.

It was liver-brown and white

She held the stuffed dog in her arms and rubbed her cheek against its snout.

'Poor old Mercury. You're loved, aren't you?' she said. 'He's a Clumber spaniel.'

'Fancy,' said Mrs Place. 'And was he a good house dog?'

'Oh yes,' said Auntie Medora. 'He used to bark and bark when someone came up the front path. He'd even bark at Jake, if he came home unexpected.'

'Ah, bless his little cotton socks,' said Mrs Place.

'He was a wedding present from my father,' said Auntie Medora.

'What a nice thought.'

Auntie Medora returned to the french windows and gazed out over the garden.

There was a small terrace immediately in front of the windows. Through the cracked stones clumps of thyme poked frizzled heads. A rosemary bush was bent to the summer sun.

'Father brought the dog by train from Wiltshire,' said Auntie Medora. 'He had to change at Crewe.'

'Fancy,' said Mrs Place.

'He was a little man with red foxy eyes and a blue pointed chin, my father,' said Auntie Medora. 'He was a very ugly man. Jake despised him. So did Thurston.'

She smiled.

'Did I ever tell you about Jake and his friend, Thurston?'

'No,' said Mrs Place. 'I don't think you ever did.'

Auntie Medora laughed.

It was a tinkly, tumbling laugh.

It was the laugh of a young and very beautiful woman.

* * *

She knows damn well she's never told me the story of Jake and Thurston.

She's never told no one as far as I know.

And do you know why?

Because there's something fishy in the woodpile.

Am I right?

I am.

She's a funniosity and no mistake.

Look at her now.

She's eyeing Garfield up now while he's on the phone like a young woman eyeing up a prospective beau.

She is.

She must have led Uncle Jake a dog's life.

Poor soul, fancy having a wife like her when she was in her prime.

'Such a nice young man, your son,' said Auntie Medora. 'So handsome.'

'Thank you,' said Mrs Place. 'That's what comes from dosing him up regular when he was little with halibut oil capsules and Ex-Lax.'

Auntie Medora looked intently at Garfield as he muttered into the phone, hunching his shoulders so that the two women could not hear what he was saying.

'Such a handsome young man,' said Auntie Medora. 'He reminds me so much of . . .'

And then she laughed her young woman's laugh and smiled her distant smile.

'I'll never forget the day we moved into the house all those years ago,' she said. 'We came round the back because we didn't want our new neighbours to see the donkey and cart with our belongings. We came round the back ginnel. Thurston had to climb over the garden wall to take the gate off the latch.

'Laugh?

'We didn't half laugh.

'The sun was blazing down but the garden was so cool. It made me shiver. It was really cool. We came into the house through the french windows. They'd left us the key, you see.

'I was so nervous when I stepped inside this room I hardly dared breathe. But Jake stepped right in and he prowled round the room as bold as brass. He was like an animal. You know how a dog quarters a strange room? It runs round the four walls and its flanks quiver. It dashes from chair to chair. It doubles back on its tracks. It's all energy. It's all action. Well, that's what Jake was like the day we moved in.'

She shook her head sadly.

But then a warm glow suffused her face, and there were vague hints of a distant beauty in the sparkle of her eyes and the tilt of her head.

She continued:

'But Thurston. Ah, Thurston was different. He was calm. He had a lovely smile on his face. So calm. Just like you, Garfield. The identical same.'

She moved to Garfield and rested her hand on his shoulder.

He flinched.

How would Hallam have coped with this situation?

Smiled, laughed, joked?

Kept quiet and popped it all into his notebook and churned it out later as a play or a story?

Much good it's done him, though.

Lying in bed all day sleeping just getting up to plough through mother's gargantuan meals.

Why could I never stand those meals?

All those mounds of food piled on your plate.

If only she'd put on a bit at a time, I could have managed.

But no, on it went. Great dollops of food, heaving and writhing on the plate and swilling in gravy.

No wonder I'm only a picker now.

It's so embarrassing when I take a client out to lunch or go to the annual functions.

My stomach just seizes up, and I can't eat a thing.

Oh hell, I hope the old lady doesn't offer me something to eat.

She will.

I know it.

If there's one thing in life I just cannot do, it's eat food prepared by very old and very ugly ladies.

'Now then,' said Auntie Medora. 'You'll no doubt be wanting something to eat, won't you?'

Before Garfield could speak his mother stepped forward and took hold of Auntie Medora's hands and squeezed them warmly.

'You're not to bother about catering for us, Auntie Medora,' she said. 'Leave us to fend for ourselves. You see, I've got Hallam lying at home in bed poorly, and we don't know how long our business is going to last, do we, love?'

'Oh, it won't take long,' said Auntie Medora.

'That's what I like to see, Auntie Medora,' said Mrs Place. 'Get your affairs in order so that those who are going to benefit from them don't have any cause to squabble amongst themselves after you've gone.

'Am I right?

'I am.'

Auntie Medora turned to Garfield and smiled, and once again beneath the stubble and the wrinkles he saw hints of smooth young flesh, rich fresh lips and smouldering eyes.

Mrs Place squeezed Auntie Medora's hands once more.

'Have no worries, Auntie Medora,' she said. 'It's very nice of you leaving us the house and all the contents, but we don't need it apart from that lovely jardiniere which will go a treat on my landing. But I can guarantee that when we sell everything after you've gone, we'll make sure it goes to a good home. Now then, if you want us to sign a chitty or . . .'

'I don't want you to sign anything, my dear,' said Auntie Medora, and she removed her hands from Mrs Place's grasp.

She walked back to the french windows, and as she stood in the light of the weak winter sun Garfield saw hints of the long lissom limbs and full firm breasts of a beautiful young woman.

She giggled.

'I think you've got everything wrong, my dear,' she said to Mrs Place.

'I beg your pardon, Auntie Medora?' said Mrs Place.

'I haven't left you the house. I haven't left the contents. That's not why I asked you here,' said Auntie Medora.

'What?' said Mrs Place and she took a step backwards and clutched at her throat.

'I've asked you here, because I want to give you something far more precious than that.'

'What, Auntie Medora?' said Mrs Place. 'What?'

'My memories,' said Auntie Medora.

'Your memories?'

'My memories,' said Auntie Medora firmly.

With that Mrs Place slowly fell backwards on to a dust-sheet covered sofa.

But in an instant she jumped up with a scream of horror, pointing to an object, on which she had sat.

Auntie Medora smiled her slow smile again and walked across to the sofa, pulled back the dust cover and lifted up a small black and white stuffed rabbit.

'There he is, Noel. I wondered where he'd got to,' said Auntie Medora. 'This is one of my memories I want you to have, my dear.'

Mrs Place sank back on to the sofa once more.

Auntie Medora fondled the rabbit with the side of her cheek.

'Memories,' she said. 'Such memories. Dear little Noel. We did love him so. Thurston bought him. Jake built a hutch for him out of weathered timber. We used to take him out of the hutch, Thurston and me, and let him run about on the lawn. He used to sit on the grass, nibbling. One afternoon we forgot we'd left him out, and the Clumber spaniel got at him and savaged him to death. You should have heard the screams. I'd like you to have him as a memory of happy days, my dear.'

She handed over the stuffed rabbit to Mrs Place.

'Thank you very much, Auntie Medora,' said Mrs Place. 'It'll come in right handy, will that.'

What did I tell you?

She's pots for rags.

Am I right?

I am.

I mean to say, she's dragged me and Garfield all the way over here on false pretences.

I mean to say, she didn't state specifically in her letter why she wanted us.

But what would you have thought?

The same as me, wouldn't you?

She's old. She's on her last legs. We're her only living relatives. So she's going to leave us all her possessions.

And now this.

Her memories.

What do I want with a stuffed rabbit?

It won't go with my furniture.

I could always use it as a doorstop, I suppose. It could always make a nice woolly toy, if our Garfield shifts himself and starts a family, which I doubt very much at the moment what with his work commitments and saving up for the mobile caravanette, but . . .

What's she up to now?

She's dragged out a tin trunk.

Words fail me. They do. They fail me.

Still, she's an old woman, I suppose.

You've got to make allowances.

And I'll tell you something else, we might get some revelations here. We might . . .

Yes. That's it. If she's spilling out her memories we might get to the bottom of Uncle Jake and Thurston.

And, in any case, we'll not go back empty-handed, will we?

I mean, if she's got another stuffed rabbit to go with this one, we'll have a pair, won't we?

And a pair is always better than one and . . .

Hello, she's opening the trunk now.

Auntie Medora opened the lid of the tin trunk and sighed with pleasure.

'All my memories are in this trunk,' she said. 'And I want you to have them.'

She stroked the flanks of the trunk slowly and sensuously.

'I remember so well the day we bought this trunk,' she said. 'There was a heat haze all morning and the swifts were screeching. We took the tram into town. We held hands on the front seat upstairs. We went to the chandler's shop at the back of the Cordwainer's Hall. Such beautiful smells there. Linseed oil. Paraffin. Turpentine and meths. I chose the trunk myself. I said to him: "I want to fill it with memories of you, so that when you're dead and buried, I'll never forget you." And he smiled and he said: "What a good idea."'

'Bless him,' said Mrs Place. 'Good old Uncle Jake.'

'Jake?' said Auntie Medora quietly. 'Jake?'

And then she returned to the trunk and pulled back a layer of oilcloth.

She looked at the contents of the trunk for quite a time, and then she pulled out a piece of paper.

'This is the receipt for the donkey and cart we used when we moved into the house,' she said. 'I'd like you to have it, Garfield.'

'My word, isn't that nice of Auntie Medora, Garfield?' said Mrs Place. 'It'll come in right handy, will that. Say thank you.'

'Thank you,' said Garfield.

Auntie Medora opened out the receipt and began to read from it.

'"Hallows and Makepeace – livery stables and carters. 139 Back Tattersall Street. For hire of one donkey and cart – two shillings and two pence."

'What memories, Garfield.

'It was a green cart.

'Its wheels were black.

'The donkey had got a cast in its right eye.

'Jake walked by its head, and Thurston walked at the back of the cart to pick up the things that dropped off.

'Happy days.

'I was such a beauty then, Garfield.

'Can you believe that?'

Garfield nodded.

'Yes,' he said. 'Yes I can.'

I can, too.

I can see it now.

I can feel her beauty.

I can touch it.

Yet it's dead and gone.

Look at her.

She's old.

She's ugly.

She's pots for rags.

God knows what else she's got in that trunk of hers.

The mind boggles.

You can hear yourself looking at her and thinking . . .

Hey.

Wait a minute.

I've been so preoccupied with this trunk and her memories that I've forgotten to ask the one crucial question – who's she left the house and its contents to?

Dear Lord above, it completely escaped my notice.

It's her influence that does it.

She always had this way of looking at you that made you feel all vague and . . . well, as though there was nothing important in life any more, that everything was trivial and didn't matter, and she sort of invaded every part of you – your mind and your body so that it was as though she was taking possession of you.

It's true.

I couldn't put a name to it when I was little, but I know it terrified me.

Mother was the same.

She used to shout at her, but underneath you could see she wasn't easy.

And neither was Uncle Jake.

I reckon that's why he . . .

No.

Take a grip on yourself.

Let's bring matters out into the open.

'I was thinking, Auntie Medora,' said Mrs Place. 'I mean, I know it's none of my business. I mean. I'm not interested either road round really, but I was sort of wondering who have you left the house and contents to, if it isn't a rude question?'

Auntie Medora looked up from the trunk.

'No,' she said. 'It's not a rude question.'

And with a laugh she returned to the trunk.

Mrs Place sniffed and flicked her shoulders.

'In that case, Auntie Medora,' she said. 'Being as how we're family, perhaps you could give us some indication as regards the beneficiaries of your will?'

'Certainly,' said Auntie Medora. 'When I die, the house and all its contents are to be sold, and the proceeds are to go to . . .'

A zoo?

She's leaving it all to a zoo?

I've never heard such nonsense in the whole of my life.

It's disgusting.

It's immoral.

Am I right?

I am.

A zoo?

Good for you, Auntie Medora.

I approve most heartily.

Why haven't I got the imagination to think of something like that?

Why do I never think of doing something daring, or frivolous, or scandalous?

I do think of thinking about it, mind you.

The trouble is I don't know how to start.

Not like Hallam.

He always had an imagination, did Hallam. I remember coming here once when we were kids, and mother sent us to play in the back garden. And Hallam said let's pretend I'm Uncle Jake and you're Thurston.

And I said who's Thurston? And Hallam said he was Uncle Jake's friend. And I said how do you know? And he said I overheard them talking. And I said how can I be someone I've never even seen? And he said use your imagination. And I said how? And he said do the same as me 'cos I've never seen Uncle Jake.

And so we played in the garden among the bushes.

It was awful.

I was hopeless.

Why couldn't I think up something like everything to a zoo?

Mother's furious.

Look at her.

She's blazing, all guns firing broadside on.

'It's disgusting, Auntie Medora.

'It's immoral.

'Am I right?

'I am.'

Mrs Place quivered with anger. Her whole body shook. Her cheeks were flushed. Her feet ground into the carpet.

Auntie Medora stared at her placidly.

There was a faint smile on Garfield's face.

'It's not that we want anything from you. Far from it. It couldn't be farthest from our mind. But if anybody's going to have anything, it should be us. We're your own flesh and blood. We're family.'

No change came to Auntie Medora's expression.

She seemed to be staring straight through Mrs Place, who continued:

'I mean, I've nothing against zoos. In context. They can be very conducive, can zoos, if you don't look too hard at what the monkeys are doing.'

Quite suddenly Auntie Medora began to laugh. It was soft laughter at first, but then it tinkled and glistened in the dusty air.

Mrs Place knotted her fists and slammed them hard against her thighs.

'Will you stop laughing while I'm talking to you,' she shouted.

Auntie Medora stopped laughing immediately.

She narrowed her eyes, and then she said:

'You're so like your mother, my dear.'

'I beg your pardon?' said Mrs Place fiercely.

'If I close my eyes and listen to you, I can hear your mother talking,' said Auntie Medora. 'Such a bully. Such a hectoring, angry, ungenerous woman. Such meanness of spirit. Such grinding, relentless humourlessness.'

There was silence.

Mrs Place's shoulders drooped. She shook her head weakly.

Auntie Medora laughed again.

She burrowed in her trunk and pulled out a large and gaudy stuffed cockatoo.

'This is Simon,' she said. 'I'd like you to have him. He's one of my most precious memories.'

She held the cockatoo at arms' length and smiled at it fondly.

'Jake loved you, didn't he, Simon?' she said. 'And so did Thurston. Thurston loved you even more, didn't he, Simon? I want you to have him, Garfield. I want you to look after him and cherish him and feed and feast off the memories he provokes in me.'

She handed the stuffed bird to Garfield.

'Thank you, Auntie Medora,' he said. 'He's lovely.'

'I know he's lovely, Garfield. He's smashing,' said Mrs Place. 'But what we've got to do now is face facts. I mean we've driven all the way here with petrol at one pound sixty three per gallon, and what's happened. We've been given a menagerie of stuffed animals. What next? What next, I say?'

'I'll show you, my dear,' said Auntie Medora. She squatted in front of the trunk and gazed inside it, but once more it was as though she were looking at objects far distant.

She ran her hands slowly over the oilskin.

'Oilskin,' she said. 'So soft. So sensuous.'

And as she spoke those words her face was suffused with the bloom of youth, and her hair glowed.

'All my memories are in this trunk,' she said slowly. 'All the most precious moments of my life. All the happiness. All the sadness. All the joy and all the misery.'

She withdrew an object from the trunk and handed it to Mrs Place.

'I particularly want you to have this, my dear,' she said.

It was a canvas knitting bag.

'Thank you very much, Auntie Medora,' said Mrs Place. 'It'll come in right handy, will this.'

'No,' said Auntie Medora. 'It's what's inside it I want you to have.'

'I see,' said Mrs Place. 'And what is inside it?'

'My baby.'

'I beg your pardon?'

'Inside that knitting bag, my dear, is the body of my baby. It's fossilized. I'd like you to have it.'

There was a pause for a moment.

And then Mrs Place spoke.

'Thank you,' she said. 'It'll come in right handy.'

Chapter Fifteen

It's not real.

It's make-believe.

It's one of Hallam's stories.

It must be.

Hallam's made it all up, and we're playing parts in it.

A fossilized baby?

Bloody hell, it's got to be make-believe.

Mrs Place peered into the knitting bag.

She nodded. She clicked her tongue. Then she closed the bag.

'Well, Auntie Medora,' she said. 'I'll say one thing for baby – he's in very good nick considering how old he is.'

'Thank you,' said Auntie Medora.

'I wonder who it takes after? It's got your nose and cheekbones, Auntie Medora, but I can't see much of Uncle Jake in him.'

Auntie Medora turned to Garfield, and she smiled her long, slow smile.

What I can't understand is why the baby's fossilized.

It's most unusual, is that.

Am I right?

I am.

Auntie Medora plunged her arm into the trunk once again and took out a small woolly object.

'Oooh, I say, Auntie Medora,' said Mrs Place.

'What a lovely little woolly bonnet. Did you knit it for baby?'

'No, my mother knit it for me when we lived in Wiltshire all those years ago,' said Auntie Medora. 'I brought it with me in my trousseau. Jake said I was daft. Jake said it was silly saving things like that. But I said it would come in handy for our baby. You should have seen Jake's face. "I'm not having no baby," he said. And I smiled at him. Oh, he did look handsome in his soldier's uniform. We were standing there in Blue Boar Row in Salisbury all those years ago. And the sun was shining. And he took me by the arm. And he said: "You're a beautiful woman, Medora," he said. And I was. I was really beautiful.'

Mrs Place patted her on the shoulder.

'You can see that, Auntie Medora, just by looking at you,' she said. 'There are still traces. There are still . . . Oooh, what's that?'

She pointed at a small square of brightly-coloured cloth inside the trunk.

Auntie Medora lifted it out and rubbed it slowly against the side of her cheek.

'That's a piece of the counterpane we had in our bedroom all those years ago, when we first moved into this house. Memories! Oh, it does bring back memories.'

'And it's in very good nick, too,' said Mrs Place. 'I'll say one thing for you, Auntie Medora – you do keep your memories in tip top condition.'

Auntie Medora turned to Garfield.

'I cherish this counterpane,' she said. 'When we were in bed together in the afternoons, we used to roll it right back.'

She paused. She smiled her smile.

'I remember one afternoon so well,' she said. 'Such a lovely afternoon. We were in the bedroom. And the counterpane was rolled back on the bed.'

* * *

I can see the scene as she describes it.

I can smell the room.

I can smell the sheets.

I can smell her body.

'I was curled up under the sheets.

'I always did after we loved.

'I used to make a little tent for myself.

'It was so cool and so tender and so loving.

'And he used to burrow his head beneath the tent.

'And he looked at me lying there naked.'

I can see her naked.

I can see her firm full breasts with the plum red nipples.

I can see her thighs.

I can see her soft brush.

'Such a strong body he had.

'Such flesh to dig your nails into.

'He kissed me in our secret place.

'And then he got out of bed and walked across the room to the window.

'So light on his feet, he was.

'So smooth his walk.

'My big handsome cat.

'He got to the windows and he pulled back the curtains.

'And the sunlight flooded in and lit up the canopy of my tent, and I felt my whole body glowing golden.'

I can see that tent.

I can see her body glowing beneath it.

I can feel the juices quicken in my loins.

Auntie Medora stood up from the trunk.

In her hands she held a large-brimmed straw hat banded in pink silk.

She put it on and walked to the french windows.

'What a lovely hat,' said Mrs Place.

'It was my favourite,' said Auntie Medora. 'I used to wear it all through the summer when I was a young woman.'

'You did right, Auntie Medora,' said Mrs Place. 'I mean to say, it would be very conducive in keeping the flies at bay, wouldn't it?'

Auntie Medora twirled round like a ballerina and fluttered her hand.

'Jake hated this hat,' she said. 'He used to say: "I hate that hat, Medora." And I used to say: "But Thurston doesn't. Thurston likes this hat," I used to say. And Jake would say: "Bugger Thurston".'

'Oooh, I say, Auntie Medora, what language! Still, men are buggers when it comes to swearing aren't they?

'Am I right?

'I am.'

Auntie Medora opened the doors of the french windows. The breeze wafted the curtains and flapped at a corner of the dust sheet over the piano.

There was a damp and corrupt smell of deep green vegetation.

'I was wearing this hat that afternoon at the back end of summer,' she said. 'The swifts had gone. He was digging in the garden. I went out to him.'

She's gone into the garden, and we've followed her. She didn't have to say anything.

We just stood up and followed her outside as though it were the most natural thing in the world.

And it was strange.

Although it was mid winter and the high trees in the distant gardens were bare, the trees and shrubs in her garden seemed to fizz and sway with life.

The dark green leaves of the holly were glowing.

And she was glowing, too.

And if you stared deep into her eyes, you could see a beautiful young woman with golden hair and long, lissom limbs.

Auntie Medora turned to Mrs Place and Garfield as they stood in the garden next to the old gnarled and tangled holly.

'How handsome he looked, my bold handsome lover,' she said.

'I went up to him. He stopped his digging and he said: "You're a beautiful woman, Medora," he said.

'And I said: "Will I grow old and ugly?" And he said: "Oh no, not you, Medora. Not you, my love".'

She moved to Garfield.

She stood close to him and looked deep into his eyes.

'My bold handsome lover,' she said softly.

A heron flapped slowly overhead, its wings hunched, its legs trailing a wake of mobbing starlings.

Auntie Medora moved even closer to Garfield.

'And then,' she said. 'And then I took him by the hand, and we went up to the bedroom, and we made love.

'Glory how we loved.'

I can feel her.

I can touch her.

I can see her in that bed.

I can feel our bodies writhing together.

I can smell the smells of love.

I can feel its thrust and its swelling and its outpourings.

Oooh, there's no need for her to go into such detail.

Not in front of Garfield.

Am I right?

I am.

I don't like hearing about things like that.

What I maintain is regarding delicate matters of that sort is this – everything in its place.

Did you see that 'Bouquet of Wire' on the BBC telly?

Disgusting.

We all know women have got unmentionables, but we don't want them ramming down our gullets, do we?

Am I right?

I am.

And look at the way she's making up to Garfield.

It's as though she thinks he's Uncle Jake with all that talk of what they did in the bedroom with no clothes on.

I think it's disgusting the way people take their clothes off these days.

Where's the beauty in the human body?

I can't stand the way everything wobbles when you move, can you?

Look at her.

She's really making up to our Garfield.

She's preening herself against him as though she was a slinky black cat.

'And when we'd finished loving and we lay side by side in bed, I told him my news,' said Auntie Medora.

A milky skein of cloud filtered over the wintry sky.

Roost-bound herring gulls yawned across the red sun's face.

The wind was chill.

Auntie Medora raised her arms and began to twirl round the garden slowly, her head thrown back, her throat arched, her palms spread upwards to the skeins of cloud.

Mrs Place and Garfield watched her silently.

They did not move.

After a while she stopped, and she laughed, and she shook her head.

‘I told Thurston I was going to have a baby,’ she said. ‘I told him it was our baby.’

Thurston’s baby?

This baby in this bag isn’t Uncle Jake’s baby?

I’ve been carrying round an illegitimate baby in this knitting bag?

The shame of it.

The disgrace.

I’ve never been so humiliated in my life.

Goodness knows what the lady in the dog biscuit shop would say, if she found out.

And I shudder to think how my foot beautician would react.

We’ve never had illegitimacy in our family, and I do not intend to start it now.

No wonder my mother hadn’t a kind word to say about Auntie Medora.

You’d only to mention the name Auntie Medora in our house, and mother would sniff three times and run the hot water tap till the boiler rattled.

It explains a lot, does this baby, poor little soul.

It explains a lot.

Am I right?

I am.

And so we follow her inside.

We’re like sheep. She doesn’t say a word. She just turns on her heel and walks back to the house, and we follow.

She motions us to sit on the sofa.

And we sit on the sofa.

She smiles her smile. She looks straight through us.

And to me she is shimmering, golden beautiful.

* * *

'When I was young and in my prime, Garfield, I was a very beautiful woman. Can you believe that?'

'Yes.'

'Jake loved me. Thurston loved me. And I loved them both. Can you believe that?'

'Yes.'

'Do you think I'm beautiful now, Garfield? Do you? Do you?'

'Yes.'

And so do I.

I don't want to, but I can't help it.

I'm looking at her as she's standing by Garfield's arm, and although she's an old lady, all I can see is a beautiful young woman.

I see her now as I used to see when I was little with adenoids and scabs on my knees.

Good Lord above, I can see her slim and youthful and beautiful and vain and cruel and dangerous.

'Jake never knew I was carrying the baby.

'I was so slim and beautiful.

'I didn't fill out at all.

'My body was as beautiful as it always was.

'Thurston waited down here in this room while I had the baby upstairs in the bedroom.

'Mrs Duckworth helped me.

'The baby was born dead.

'The first thing Thurston said to me when he came into the room was: "My God, Medora, you're a beautiful woman."

'He was so tired and he stretched himself on the bed beside me and I cradled his head in my arms and he fell asleep.

'Jake came home unexpected and found him there.

'He stood there in the door and he looked down on us and he never said a word.

'And I said: "Hullo, Jake".'

She smiled to herself.

She moved to the trunk and took out a small, thin leather case.

'This is another of my memories,' she said. 'I'd like you to have it.'

She opened the case and picked out a cut throat razor.

'This belonged to Jake,' she said. 'He used it when he had his accident.'

And in an instant I know what mother said to her.

I do.

I'm looking at her now and I can hear what mother said to her in this very room all those years ago.

Ooh, it's right sinister, is this.

I mean, I wasn't even there.

And when I grew up, mother never told me what she said.

It's those eyes of hers. The way she stares at you. It eats into your brain. It bores into your memories.

It destroys time.

It plays tricks with it.

Those eyes and that smile – and I can hear myself speaking mother's words all those years ago. They went like this:

'I'm Jake's sister, and I intend to make it my business, Medora, that you and Thurston will never ever for the rest of your lives be able to forget what you did to him.

'You'll grow old, Medora.

'You'll grow ugly.

'You'll grow senile and ga ga, but never for one single moment will you be able to forget what you did to my brother.

'You may well squirm, Thurston.

'Judas!

'He thought the world of you, did Jake. He'd have done anything for you, would Jake. He took you into his own home. He comforted you. He cossetted you. And what did you do?

'You carried on with his wife while he was out working to keep house and home together. You gave his wife a baby. And he came home and found you in bed with her.

'I loathe you.

'I despise you.

'I always have done.'

Dear God, it's as though I'm talking to Garfield.

While I'm saying them words to myself it's as though I'm really addressing them to Garfield.

And I can't stop myself.

'Beautiful, Medora.

'Young, slim, willowy Medora.

'Your husband's dead.

'He slit his throat.

'Well, don't worry, love.

'I'll not tell the bobbies.

'I'll not tell a living soul.

'But there's just one condition – you get rid of Thurston.'

She's narrowing her eyes at me.

It's as though she can hear what I'm saying.

It's as though she's hearing those words my mother said to her all those years ago.

And Garfield?

Garfield's reacting, too.

It's got to stop.

But I can't.

That smile of hers. Those eyes.

'Get shut of Thurston now. That's the price you're going to pay. Get rid of him, and your secret will be safe.'

I feel real hatred to her.

I can feel it boiling in my veins and curdling and writhing and . . .

Ooh, it's awful.

Honest.

And I can't control it. I can't help myself.

'You'll grow so old and so ugly, Medora, you'll despise yourself.

'You'll grow into the ugliest woman in the world. People will turn their heads away from you.

'People will run from you.

'But you won't be able to run.

'You'll be trapped deep inside your ugliness.'

Auntie Medora stared intently at Mrs Place and shook her head slowly.

'So like your mother you are,' she said. 'Glory, how like your mother you are.'

Mrs Place glared back at her.

Then suddenly she stood up and threw the cut throat razor at her feet.

'Keep it,' she said. 'And the rest of your memories. We don't want anything to do with them. Keep them for yourself.'

She motioned to Garfield and obediently he followed her to the door.

Auntie Medora did not move.

She just said softly:

'That's just how Thurston left all those years ago.'

I know it is.

And I know what he said to her, too.

I can hear myself saying: 'You've always been old and ugly to me, Medora. Not the way you look. It's the way you feel, the way you act. That's where you're old and ugly, Medora.

'You always have been. You always will be.

'When you're an old woman in this house living on your own and all your friends and relations are dead, that's the time you'll really flower and blossom.

'When you can't harm no one no more, that's when you'll be young and beautiful.'

Mrs Place and her son, Garfield, walked down the front path of the house.

When they paused briefly and looked back both of them were convinced they saw a beautiful young woman staring at them from the attic window.

Both of them were convinced she waved to them and blew them a kiss.

And Garfield was certain he saw the figure of a young man standing in the shadows behind her.

Chapter Sixteen

Old people!

They're all the same, aren't they?

Running noses, hollow chests and always spilling their loose change in the post office.

If I get like that, I want them to put me down.

I do.

Look at Auntie Medora.

Do you know when we got into Garfield's car, I discovered I'd still got that knitting bag.

I was going to take it back, but Garfield said no, so I didn't.

I looked inside, however.

And do you know what?

There was no baby there.

Isn't that typical?

I wonder if we imagined it all.

It's like during the war when you queued for two hours solid in the butchers and when you got to the counter, you found out he'd run out of ox liver.

I used to say to myself then – I must have imagined it all.

Garfield thinks that it was Hallam who dreamed it all up.

I wouldn't put it past him.

He was always a dreamer, was Hallam.

It used to say so on his school reports.

It used to say: 'Geography. If Hallam were to concentrate more and show greater application, he could make progress in this subject – J. J. K. Winterbottom BA (Sheffield).'

It was the same in religious instruction and difficult sums.

But in English he always excelled.

That's where his dreaming came in handy, you see, because it helped him make up stories for his essays and his compositions.

I will say this for them at the grammar – they gave him every encouragement.

They did.

They taught him how to swim. They taught him how to play the recorder. They taught him knots in their scout troop.

He was no good at sports, though, wasn't Hallam.

It wasn't that he'd no interest.

He had.

He went to all the matches. He read all the reports. And you'd only to give him cigarette cards of famous cricketers of the past, and he'd be away for slates.

He just did not like playing games.

And that was somewhat of a handicap at the grammar.

They were very keen on games at the grammar.

Their first team colours were black, green and cerise hoops when they played rugby.

Hallam used to go to all the matches.

I didn't. I couldn't abide Madame running up and down the touchline bawling her head off like that.

So unladylike.

Still, that was typical.

She certainly wasn't an asset.

Poor Mr Garlick.

Fancy having a wife like that, and him so gentle and cultured and well-mannered.

The school's never been the same since he retired as headmaster.

Am I right?

I am.

If he'd still been head, they'd never have gone

comprehensive with all those little darkies riding their bikes with no hands.

He wouldn't have allowed a darkie to darken his doorstep wouldn't Mr Garlick.

He would not.

I was only talking about it with him the other night, when we went to . . .

The other night?

That's a story, I can tell you.

What it was, you see, was this – the Old Boys Association wanted to make a presentation to Mr Garlick, and as it was twenty-five years to the very day since the sixth formers of the boys and girls grammars had organized a dance, they thought they'd organize another dance for all the old boys and old girls and invite Mr Garlick along as guest of honour so they could give him his present.

I suppose that's as clear as mud, is it?

Never mind.

There's nothing simple about life these days, is there?

That's why you've got to have God and David Jacobs on Any Questions.

Am I right?

I am.

Where was I?

I know – the anniversary dance.

Well, as you can imagine, Hallam didn't want to go.

Garfield and his wife, Hazel, did. They were all for it. Well, they met at the dance twenty-five years ago, so it was a sort of celebration for them, wasn't it?

But as for Hallam – he just turned his nose up at it and made remarks.

Well, I wasn't having that.

On your hind legs, I said, and go. It'll do you good meeting all your old pals after living in that flat in Wimbledon for so long. It'll take your mind off Shirley. It'll be therapeutic and as I'm responsible for the catering, you'll get first choice of cakes.

You should have seen the look he gave me.

Any road, to cut a long story short he decided to go.

Mind you, I know why. I've no illusions about his motives. He's going to write it all up in his little notebook and then he'll use it to make fun of us in one of his plays.

Still, I was thankful for small mercies.

At least it would get him out of the house.

But, of course, knowing Hallam, he had to have his final word.

On the night of the dance he came downstairs from his bedroom and you should have seen what he was wearing.

Honest to God, he looked like a rag-riser.

White pumps, blue jeans and one of those sweat shirt thingies.

He looked a sight.

But there's no telling him.

He thinks it's clever dressing like that.

But I think it shows a person up.

Don't you?

Chapter Seventeen

On the night of the anniversary dance at the grammar Hallam Place had been staying with his mother for three months.

Spring had arrived.

The shovellers and pintail had left the damp-eyed municipal lakes.

There were midges and daffodils.

The buds of lilac were fat.

The softening skies waited for the first of the swallows.

Hallam Place looked at himself in the mirror on the dressing table in his bedroom.

He winked at his reflection.

Then he picked up his small blue notebook and his ball point pen and slipped them out of sight into the hip pocket of his jeans.

He winked at himself again and then he went downstairs to join his mother in her drawing room.

'Howdie,' he said.

Mrs Place turned to him and gave a small gasp of horror.

'Hallam! You're never going to a dance in white plimsolls?' she said. 'You look like a rag-riser, lad. You'll make a holy show of me. Now go upstairs this minute and put a suit on and your university tie.'

Hallam Place took his mother by the arm and led her to the door.

'Come on,' he said. 'It's time we were collecting Garfield and Hazel.'

I wonder if old man Garlick will turn up?

It would be typical of him not to. Oh yes, he'd say, I'd love to come to the dance, my dears. How honoured I am that you would want me to be your guest of honour. A presentation? My dears, the joy, the anticipation.

And then he wouldn't turn up. Or maybe he'd die.

A nice touch.

I remember so clearly that morning after the dance all those years ago.

We were sitting in the sixth form room and he shuffled in trailing his tattered, chalky gown like a funeral train and clicking his tongue and chuckling to himself.

And he said:

'Gentlemen of the Upper and Lower Sixth – good morning to you, my dears.

'And did we all enjoy the school dance last night? I trust we did. Madame was telling me over breakfast that never had she seen such a collection of glum and cavernous faces.

'Madame said to me: "Girls. Don't the chaps like girls?"'

'Well, my dears? What answer do I give her? Is Madame right? Don't you like girls?'

Some of us tittered. Some of us groaned inwardly. Some of us stared at him stonily.

'Fallows, you're head boy,' he said. 'Kindly speak out on behalf of your colleagues in the Upper and Lower Sixth.'

'Well, sir,' said Fallows. 'It's . . . It's . . .'

'Don't "well, sir" me, Fallows,' said Mr Garlick. 'I can't stand iffers and butters. Be incisive in thought and deed – that's the secret. Your answer if you please.'

Fallows, the daft pompous twat, stood up and gripped the lapels of his blazer and said:

'I think some of the chaps like girls, sir. And some of them don't.'

Mr Garlick threw up his arms and clapped his hands high above his head.

'Bravo, my dear,' he said. 'That is the answer of a man who will go far in life.'

And then he tried to take the piss out of me, and failed.

And then he tried to take the piss out of Garfield, and succeeded.

And then young Tattersall from the second form came in with a message and got so confused he forgot what to say and Garlick dismissed him spikily in a flood of tears.

What a prize bastard.

Hallam Place and his mother collected Garfield and his wife, Hazel, and set off for the school, where the dance and presentation were to be held.

Hallam looked at Hazel in the driving mirror.

She was wearing an orange flared skirt with a broad leather belt. Her shirt-waister blouse had three-quarter length sleeves, turned back winged cuffs and a deep cleavage.

Hallam smiled.

'I hope you're wearing your grope-proof bra, Hazel,' he said.

'Hallam!' said Mrs Place. 'What a disgusting thing to say. Pay him no heed, Hazel.'

'I never do,' said Hazel and she smiled back at Hallam, and he winked.

Mrs Place leaned forward from the back seat and prodded Hallam Place on the back of the neck.

'You're on a very sticky wicket making comments about how people are dressed, young man,' she said. 'You should take a leaf out of Garfield's book.'

'Mother, leave it alone,' said Garfield wearily.

'I will not leave it alone, Garfield,' said Mrs Place. 'There's you dressed in a smart navy blue blazer and grey flannel trousers and there's your brother dressed like a rag and bone man.'

'That's the bohemian look, mother,' said Hazel calmly.

'I am well aware of that, Hazel,' said Mrs Place. 'But he's

not in Bohemia now. That's the whole point.'

Hallam winked at Hazel again, and she smiled and showed him the tip of her tongue.

She's a smashing girl, is Hazel.

She's a lovely girl to have as a daughter-in-law.

She's made a lovely home for Garfield.

It's spotless.

You'd have to be a real tartar to find fault with her table linen and she does a beautiful salad for Sunday tea with her lettuce always immaculately washed.

That's precisely the sort of girl I always wanted Hallam to marry.

She'd have been an asset to him, you see.

I don't care what your line of business is, you must have a wife who'll be an asset to you.

Every man must have a wife he can take out in company in the certain knowledge she'll not make a show of him by drinking pints of beer and talking too loud in a loud voice.

Hallam swung the car through the school gates and brought it to a halt in front of the main entrance.

Just before they went inside Hazel threw her arms round Garfield and said:

'I love you.'

'Don't,' said Garfield. 'Not here.'

Hazel smiled and kissed him full on the lips.

'And remember,' she said. 'If the head does turn up tonight, don't let him bully and humiliate you. Right? Stand up to him. Do you hear me, Garfield? Stand up to him.'

Hallam paused for a moment and stared at the sandy-bricked façade of the school.

A kestrel was hovering.

Starlings scuttered in the gutters.

* * *

Bloody hell, it's amazing.

I can still remember that morning after the dance.

Old man Garlick was so smug. He bounced up and down on the balls of his heels. He smirked. He clicked his tongue and chuckled to himself.

And then he said:

'My dears, I propose to assign you a task this morning.'

We groaned the ritual groan.

He smirked the ritual smirk.

'As a result of certain childish behaviour displayed by certain members of this form at the dance last night I intend to set you a childish task. A composition.'

We groaned again.

'And its title?' he said with a bounce and a chuckle. 'Its title will be "What I will Be in Twenty-Five Years' Time." Quite perfect don't you think, chaps? Does it appeal to you, Place Junior?'

Poor Garfield spluttered and blushed.

'Iffers and butters, Place Junior, iffers and butters. In twenty-five years' time, my dear, will you still be iffing and butting?'

'No, sir,' said Garfield.

Another chuckle. Another swish of the hem of the gown.

'I know what's in store for you, Place Junior.'

'Sir?' said Garfield.

'In twenty-five years' time you will be married to the attractive young lady in the orange skirt you met at the dance last night.'

The idiots banged their desk lids with glee.

Suckers. Played right into his lap.

'Silence. Silence,' he screamed with superbly simulated anger.

And, of course, the suckers fell silent. And, of course, he chuckled.

He moved forward to Garfield's desk and rested his elbows upon it.

‘Will you have a nice suburban house on a nice suburban estate, Place Junior?’ he said. ‘Will you have a through lounge/diner and integral waste disposal? With a neat little garden with phlox and lilies and wallflowers and pansies and marigolds and roses?

‘Roses?

‘Ah yes, Place Junior, suburban roses.

‘Rows and rows of suburban roses.’

You sham.

You third-rate, evil buffoon.

When Hallam went inside the school, he discovered his brother, Garfield, reading the notices on the board in the foyer.

‘All right, mate?’ he said.

Garfield nodded.

‘Just look at this,’ he said, pointing to a type-written form on the board.

Hallam Place read it out loud.

‘“All pupils are reminded that it is an offence – repeat offence – to park their motor cycles in places reserved for members of staff.”’

He raised his eyebrows, and Garfield shook his head gloomily.

‘Some of them bring their cars to school these days,’ he said. ‘Times have changed.’

‘You can say that again,’ said Hallam Place. ‘They’ve probably turned the bike sheds into an official brothel for the sixth form.’

They’re playing Victor Sylvester in the hall.

Okay, fans, who’s the leader of the Victor Sylvester Ballroom Orchestra, strictly strict tempo, my dears?

Answer – Oscar Grasso.

All those who got it right, go to the top of the form.

Twenty-five years ago?

The notices on the board have changed, but everything else is the same.

The same green paintwork. The same scuffed tiles. The same smell of ink and chalk and sweaty socks and cheap paper.

And the people?

Hardly changed at all.

The waists are thicker. The breasts are plumper. The jaws are jowled and the necks are wrinkled.

But the eyes are the same. The set of the mouth is the same.

Mediocrity can never be changed.

And Hazel?

What if I'd re-written the story twenty-five years ago and taken up her offer?

What now?

A wife, a lounge/diner, integral waste disposal and rows and rows and rows of suburban roses?

No Wimbledon. No Shirley. No Wilfred.

So?

Does it really matter?

Hazel walked through the swing doors, which led to the corridors of the west wing and the dining room and the kitchen.

She looked round the foyer and spotted her husband and his brother reading notices on the board.

She went up to them and linked their arms.

'Well, my bold lads, your mother's happy at long last,' she said. 'The tea urn's gurgling away. She's bossing Mrs Philipson. She's gossiping with Mrs Pollard. She's . . .'

She stopped and cocked her head to one side.

'Victor Sylvester!' she said. 'Crikey, I haven't heard him for ages. Isn't it wonderful?'

'Great,' said Garfield. 'Do you fancy a dance?'

Hallam Place smiled.

'First things first, Garfield,' he said. 'How about slipping out to the pub for a quick one?'

'Great idea,' said Garfield, 'Yes, Hazel?'

'Well, just for a quickie,' said Hazel.

Hallam Place rested his hand on her bottom.

The cheeks were firm and smooth and rounded.

'A quickie?' he said. 'That brings back memories.'

Hazel brushed away his hand.

'Yes, my dear,' she said. 'But this time we're talking about the pub.'

Is she happy with things?

Mrs Junior Executive in a Shirt Manufacturing Company?

Mrs Lounge/Diner?

Mrs Integral Waste Disposal?

Mrs Suburban Roses?

How would she have made out in Wimbledon?

Well, for a start off, Wilfred would have been clipped.

And there would have been no . . .

Oh, my God, J. A. Fallows!

He's coming over.

He's bearing in on me.

Hazel!

You bitch!

She's whisked herself away with Garfield and I'm on my own.

Hallam Place versus Mr Mediocrity in person.

J. A. Fallows grasped Hallam Place's hand with two firm, crunching hands.

His skin was sallow and heavy. His hair was receding at the temples. He wore a fob watch and an Old Boys tie and a small badge in the left lapel of his blue suit.

'Well then, Place,' he said. 'They tell me you've made a go of things writing comedy for television.'

'I've not done too badly,' said Hallam Place.

Two stout ladies in black velvet skirts and white blouses entered the dance hall. There was a brief blast of Guy Mitchell.

'I watch very little television myself, Place. I'm far too busy for that sort of thing,' said J. A. Fallows. 'Mind you, what little comedy I do watch is absolute rubbish. Now if you want a really original idea for a comedy series, you want to have a chat with me.'

'Really?'

'Certainly,' said J. A. Fallows and he ran his fingers along the chain of his fob watch. 'I've said it before and I'll say it again – it's high time there was a comedy series written about my line of business.'

'And what is your line of business?'

'Pre-stressed concrete.'

'Ah,' said Hallam Place.

'The funny stories I could tell you about the pre-stressed concrete business. They'd have you falling about, Place.'

Twenty-five years ago you were still a big soft prat, J. A. Fallows.

Garlick knew it.

I watched him out of the corner of my eye as we wrote our essays.

'What I Shall Be in Twenty-Five Years' Time' – nice one, Mr Garlick.

He preened himself as he walked from desk to desk, pausing occasionally to read silently from the work of one of his victims.

And he chuckled to himself and stroked his chin and clicked his tongue and nodded contentedly.

He stopped in front of J. A. Fallows.

J. A. Fallows – prize berk, future rotarian, local councillor, independent ratepayer, hon. sec. old boys association, father of three children all receiving private education, big noise in the pre-stressed concrete industry.

He wrote with laborious concentration in that smug, small, neat hand-writing.

'Such industry, Fallows,' said Mr Garlick. 'And what, my dear, have you written?'

J. A. Fallows looked up from his work with a start.

'Well, sir, I . . . I . . .' he spluttered.

'Let me guess what you have written, Fallows,' said Mr Garlick. He stroked his chin thoughtfully, furrowed his brow, scratched his head and pretended to think long and deeply.

At length he said:

'I know, Fallows. You will have written of your adventures – the sensuous mysteries of Paris, the bawdy excesses of Hamburg, the . . .'

'Now hold on, sir,' said J. A. Fallows.

'Do not interrupt.'

'Sorry, sir.'

Titters.

Sniggers.

'You will have written, Fallows, of your travels to Samarkand and Katmandu, to Kashgar and Shanghai, to the silken souks of Araby. You will have written of revels in the tropic isles of the South Seas with coral beaches, swaying palms and dusky maidens.'

Laughter.

Banging of desk lids.

Triumph on the face of our headmaster.

You bad old bugger, Garlick.

Hallam Place interrupted J. A. Fallows as he was about to

lumber into an account of his amusing experiences as chairman of the Independent Ratepayers Association.

'Look,' he said. 'I think I'll be nipping along into the hall.'

'No,' said J. A. Fallows. 'I've got other plans for you.'

'You what?' said Hallam Place. 'What the bloody hell do you mean – "other plans"?'

'It's quite all right, Place. Calm down. Everything's all right in the hall. Mr Ullapool is working the gramophone and . . .'

'Ullapool? You've invited Ullapool after what had happened twenty-five years ago at the dance?'

'I don't bear grudges, Place. I grant you that his incident with Madame at the dance nearly . . .'

'What are these plans you've got for me?' said Hallam Place sharply.

'It's old man Garlick,' said J. A. Fallows. 'He's in a bit of a state. He's in the sixth form study at the moment, and he refuses to come out.'

'So?'

'So I want you to go and have a chat with him and winkle him out.'

'Why me?'

'Because he always had a soft spot for you.'

'Bollocks.'

'Now there's no need for foul language, Place,' said J. A. Fallows. 'That's the whole trouble with television these days, if you don't mind me saying so. Far too much swearing and nudity and general immorality. Now we on the Independent Ratepayers Association recently passed a motion condemning in no uncertain terms the BBC's lack of . . .'

'See you,' said Hallam Place, and he turned on his heel, pushed open the door which led to the corridors of the east wing and headed for the sixth form study.

It hasn't changed.

Same dim lights. Same green doors. Same inward opening windows.

'Would you nip next door to Mr Ullapool, Place Senior, and ask if I can borrow the window pole?'

Same sandy bricks, flaking and crumbling.

And old man Garlick?

Has he changed?

Open the door of the sixth form study.

Enter.

There he is, behind his desk, snoozing softly.

Dear God, he hasn't changed a bit.

Same laughter lines at the corners of the eyes. Same tight mouth. Same bald pate. Same smooth-stroked chin.

The never changing geography of malice.

Hallam Place walked softly to the desk and tapped Mr Garlick on the shoulder.

He awoke with a pained little grunt.

And then he smiled.

'Just resting, Place. Just taking a snooze,' he said. 'A small rehearsal for death.'

Hallam Place nodded.

'And how are you keeping, Place Senior?'

'I'm well.'

'You always were. Not like me. I'm a sick man, Place. I wake up in the morning, and I've pains in the tops of the arms, I can't swallow, I've pains in the chest, weakness in the legs. I need to belch all the time. I shuffle. I slur my words. My heart feels as though it's awash in saliva. I'm a sick man, Place.'

Hallam Place nodded.

He edged his way through the row of desks. He found his old desk. He sat down.

Mr Garlick watched him, his eyes glinting.

'I have a cure for my sickness, Place,' he said. 'Can you guess what it is.'

'No.'

'Wine.'

'What?'

'Wine, my dear. Red wine. The Spaniards of the interior drink red wine at breakfast. So do I. It rids me instantly of my sickness. I drink it constantly. The slightest hint of pains in the arms, or twinges in the heart and out comes the red wine.'

He took a large silver hip flask from his jacket pocket and held it up.

'A blessed relief, Place. A profound comfort.'

He took a swig from the flask, smacked his lips and sighed with contentment.

'This morning, Place, I found a dead bat on the lawn,' he said.

'Ah,' said Hallam Place.

'I went out to sniff the air, and there it was. A dead bat, lying on its back, its front legs drawn up beneath its chin, its face screwed up in rage.

'It looked absolutely livid, Place.

'And then I found another.

'And another and another and another.

'It was a family of bats, my dear. All dead on the lawn. They looked furious about it.

'Madame looked furious after she died. Did you know Madame had passed on, Place?'

'No.'

'She died under most unfortunate circumstances. You see, Place, my life's work has been the compilation of a monograph, entitled "The Cricket Pavilions of England and Wales." We were halfway through it, I writing the essays, Madame providing the watercolours.

'So sad.

'She died during the luncheon adjournment at Hinckley.

'Leicestershire 87 for the loss of three wickets.'

The corners of his eyes crinkled, and his shoulders began to rock.

'She looked furious in the mortuary, Place. Absolutely livid. When they put the lid on her coffin, her face was contorted with rage. She was absolutely furious.'

Hallam Place coughed.

Mr Garlick beamed broadly.

'I hear you're making quite a name for yourself in the world of television, Place.'

'I'm doing all right.'

Mr Garlick belched.

'I am a television addict, Place,' he said.

'Really?'

'Oh yes. I watch a great deal of television. Do you know what my favourite television programme is, Place?'

Here we go. The start of the game. Taking the piss.

Not with me, matey.

You couldn't do it then. You can't do it now.

'I was asking, Place, if you could guess what my favourite television is.'

'No, I can't.'

'When they blow up cooling towers and mill chimneys. And then they show it again in slow motion, and then they run the film backwards so it appears the towers and chimneys are rising from death and destruction and being restored to life. Do you enjoy programmes like that, Place?'

Don't.

It won't work.

'There should be infinitely more programmes like that on the box, don't you think, Place?'

I said, don't play that game with me. I'm too old for it. Too wise. Too tired.

'I really think you should use your influence, Place, to get more programmes like that on our television screens. You do have influence, don't you, my dear?'

'What do you think?'

He took out his flask of wine and took a long draught. He wiped his mouth on his sleeve and belched long and loud.

'What do I think, Place?' he said. 'Oh, I think you have profound influence, my dear. I think you have access to all the people "who matter". Tell me secrets about the people "who matter", Place. Tell me about the home life of our own dear Mr Barry Took. Tell me about the inner fears and secret doubts of Mr Phil Drabble. Is Mr Billy Cotton half the man his father was?'

It is no longer funny.

It is a worn-out game, and I will not play it with you.

'A writer! How I envy you, Place,' said Mr Garlick and he leaned back in his chair and placed his hands behind his head. 'You can create, and you can destroy. Birth, death, destruction – yours to dispose of as you will. How wonderful. Tell me, Place, if you had the power to devise a suitable end for me, what would you choose?'

Don't tempt me, matey.

There are so many ends I could write for you.

What you really need, my dear, is a mediocre death.

An exceptionally mediocre death.

Mr Garlick took another swig of his flask and then he stood up and began to shuffle about the room.

He fingered the desks. He ran the palms of his hands over the walls. He breathed in deeply.

'The old smells, Place,' he said. 'Old familiar smells – chalk, dry ink, pencil sharpeners, sour milk, perspiration. Masses and masses of perspiring pubescent bodies.'

He raised his arms above his head and pirouetted very slowly.

'I can smell the smells of that dance twenty-five years

ago,' he said. 'Sticky haircream. Sweaty feet. Stale armpits. Stale crutches. Stale breath. The smell of corruption. The smell of death.'

Suddenly he dropped his arms and spun round to face Hallam Place.

'Do you remember Mr Ullapool, Place?'

'Yes.'

'Mr Ullapool had exceptionally clammy hands, Place. Did you know that?'

'No.'

'I used to lie awake at nights and think about Mr Ullapool and his exceptionally clammy hands. I used to think – he'll be with a woman now. He was extremely fond of the opposite sex, our Mr Ullapool. Did you know that, Place?'

'Yes.'

'As I lay in bed I used to imagine Mr Ullapool with his woman. I could see him quite plainly. Naked. And he'd be pawing the naked body of his female companion. And I'd think to myself – how dreadful it must be for her that moment when her breasts are enclosed by a pair of exceptionally clammy hands.'

He chuckled and pirouetted slowly once more.

'Madame danced with him all night, Place, at that dance twenty-five years ago. They were so shameless. And you all stood there and stared at them and snickered and sniggered and . . . why have you come here, Place?'

'I've been asked to take you into the hall.'

'The hall, Place?'

'For the dance. Fallows wants you to meet the guests.'

'Fallows! An exceptionally nauseating and disgusting youth, our J. A. Fallows. Whatever became of him, Place?'

'He's something big in pre-stressed concrete.'

Mr Garlick nodded.

He picked up the window pole and began to stroke it softly, chuckling to himself.

'And your brother, Place?' he said. 'Whatever became of him?'

'He's in the hall now. Ask him yourself.'

'Dear old Place Junior,' said Mr Garlick, and he belched softly again and held his right hand to his heart. 'What an exceptionally agreeable boy he was. What a splendid chef he would have made on a British Rail dining car. Or possibly a salesman of bathroom furniture. Or a dental mechanic or a dramatic critic on the *Manchester Guardian* – that sort of thing. Whatever has your brother made of himself, Place?'

'Don't you remember what you forecast for him?'

'No, Place, I don't think I do.'

You do, you bastard. You remember it perfectly.

But I'll tell you.

This part of the game I do not mind playing.

'Twenty-five years ago on the day after the school dance you stood where you're standing now and my brother was sitting at that desk in front of you and you asked him . . .'

'I asked him what was to become of him in twenty-five years time. Am I right, Place?'

'Yes.'

'I asked him if he would be married to the young lady he met at the dance. I asked him if he would have a nice suburban house on a nice suburban estate with a nice little garden with neat little roses. Suburban roses. Rows and rows and rows of suburban roses. Is that correct, Place?'

'It is.'

'And what has become of him?'

'The poor sod lives in a nice little house on a nice little estate with rows and rows and rows of suburban roses, and he's married to the girl he met at the dance.'

Mr Garlick threw back his head and bellowed with laughter.

He raised his arms and clapped his hands.

And then he began to cough. His face turned scarlet as he spluttered and wheezed. His chest heaved. He gasped for breath.

At length he took out a handkerchief and wiped his nose and his chin.

He took a long slow drink from his flask of wine and he belched and he smiled.

'Success. Fulfilment,' he said. 'My life's work realized, Place. I've created a happy ending.'

He offered his flask to Hallam Place.

'No thank you.'

He shuffled back to his desk and sat down heavily in the chair.

'When Madame and I first saw this school when it was being built in 1939, she turned to me and she said: "I intend to make this a school for young gentlemen." "But, Madame," I said. "This is a grammar school. It is public schools which turn out young gentlemen." She turned to me and she said in that dear hectoring voice of hers: "Stuff and nonsense. It is the duty of a grammar school to produce young gentlemen. That is its sole purpose. And that is what we shall do – produce young gentlemen who will wear striped blazers, Oxford bags and straw boaters in the summer and black toppers in the winter. They will play rugger and form string quartets. They will become statesmen and poets. They will become distinguished amateur sportsmen and Conservative politicians. And, above all, they will become young gentlemen."

'And then, Place, the war came, and then the peace came, and then we had austerity, and all her plans were destroyed. Curious, is it not, that a woman of such coarseness and vulgarity should have made plans of such refinement and delicacy?'

'Yes.'

'You knew, of course, how vulgar she was?'

'Yes.'

'You all made jokes about her.'

'Yes.'

'You knew about her affairs with members of my staff, and you mocked her?'

'Yes.'

He smiled.

'Well, that, my dear, is why I dedicated my whole life to getting my own back on you.'

'I don't follow.'

Mr Garlick laughed and coughed and took another drink of his wine.

'She was a beautiful woman, Madame, was she not, Place?'

'Yes.'

'Dark, smouldering black hair. Full bold lips. Straight nose with flared nostrils. And such a bosom. She had a magnificent bosom, did she not, Place?'

'Yes.'

'Do you remember Young Tattersall?'

'Yes.'

'A timid little boy, young Tattersall. One day I caught him in flagrante delicto. He was in the toilets drawing a picture of Madame on the wall. A naked Madame. An exceedingly naked Madame. And alongside her was an equally naked Mr Ullapool.

'Young Tattersall did not see me, Place. I allowed him to complete his work. I hid behind one of the pillars outside the biology lab, and when he left the toilet, I went inside and inspected his handiwork. I looked at it long and hard. And then I summoned the caretaker, and I said: "Makepeace, under no circumstances must this drawing be removed from the wall." And it wasn't.

'Ah, Place, how they mocked me, those boys. How they snickered and sniggered. Silly boys. I had my revenge on them. And why?

'Because, my dear, I dedicated my life into turning every single one of them into a thundering mediocrity.'

* * *

Yes.

Now I remember.

The day after the dance.

He stood in front of us and pirouetted slowly and coughed.

'How goes it with our essays, my dears?' he said. 'Do they prosper?'

We muttered and snickered.

'And what dreams have they unlocked in you, chaps? Rich dreams or mediocre dreams?'

He turned to Garfield and began to knead his shoulder gently.

'What about your dreams, my dear? Rich or mediocre?'

Garfield blushed and lowered his head.

Garlick chuckled and kneaded Garfield's shoulder more firmly.

'I see your future so clearly, Place Junior,' he said. 'Marriage to that lovely young lady you met at the dance last night. A neat house on a neat estate. Neat children. A neat job with a neat car and a neat secretary. A life of neatness, Place Junior. Does that appeal to you, my dear?'

'I wouldn't mind a life like that, sir,' said Garfield.

Garlick stood back from him, and his whole face was beaming with pleasure.

'Say it again,' he said.

Garfield licked his lips and looked around at us helplessly.

Then he said in a low voice:

'I wouldn't mind a life of neatness, sir.'

Garlick raised his arms above his head and clapped his hands.

'Bravo,' he cried. 'Bravo. My dear, Place Junior. You are my first mediocrity. What fulfilment. What bliss.'

Hallam Place watched Mr Garlick as he drank more wine.

He watched him silently as he stood up from his desk and

began to pad round the room once more.

He stood in front of a group photograph, faded and fly-blown and ran his fingers across it, calling out the names of the boys.

'Statham, Duckworth, Parkin, Greenhough, Dyson. All mediocrities. You didn't stand a chance at the grammar, my dears.'

He turned to Hallam Place.

'Statham is no longer with us, Place.'

'No?'

'He's dead. Poor chap. A climbing accident on Kinder Scout. Such a mediocre hill, my dear.'

He grinned and turned back to the group photograph.

'But all the rest are with us,' he said. 'Duckworth, Parkin, Greenhough, Dyson. What peaks of achievement they've reached. Positive Kinder Scouts, my dear. Tennis club romeos. Snug bar braggarts. Golf club lechers. Washers of Sunday morning cars. Pushers of supermarket trolleys. Drivers of mobile caravanettes. Family butchers, salesmen of second-hand cars, junior executives, teachers of chemistry, chartered surveyors, exceptionally civil engineers. Dead black bats on a lush green lawn.'

Slowly he turned.

'But not you, Place,' he said. 'Not you, my dear. You are unique. Priceless. A1. You are the one who got away.'

His eyes slanted for a moment. His mouth tightened. His brow furrowed.

And then he smiled.

'You got away from me, Place. My one failure,' he said. 'How I remember that essay you wrote twenty-five years ago. Magnificent. So clever. So accurate in its forecast.

'Would you rewrite it now, Place? If you had the chance would you rewrite the past? What power you have, my dear. Use it now. Use it now and rewrite the past.'

Silently Hallam Place stood up.

He walked to the door and opened it.

'It's time to go to the hall,' he said.

Mr Garlick nodded and meekly followed him out into the corridor.

Well, you've probably been wondering where I've been all this time.

Am I right?

I am.

I'll tell you.

I've been slaving away in the kitchens supervising the preparation of the running buffet.

Honestly, some women have no idea, have they?

That Mrs Duckworth – she's brought a load of home-made sausage rolls.

Now I'm not saying anything against them as such, but I never have been a lover of puff pastry, and where she got the sausages from to use as fillings I just do not know.

I think she must have been round the knacker's yard.

And what about that Mrs Dyson?

Dyed blonde hair and black roots.

Talk about mutton dressed as lamb.

And she's done nothing but play her transistor full blast.

The last straw was when the Nolan Sisters came on.

What a shower?

I'm not a prejudiced person, but if I had my way I'd deport them back to Ireland and let them inflict their singing on their own sort.

What we've done to deserve it, I do not know.

Anyway, I'm taking a breather now.

I've done more than my fair share.

I'm in the hall, stood just inside the door, watching them dance.

Oh, it is a nice sight.

None of the twist and shake stuff like they do on Top of the Pops.

It's nice graceful ballroom dancing like they used to do on the television in the days before Peter West got too big for his boots.

Isn't it lovely to see them all together?

I bet Mr Garlick will be really proud when he sees them.

They do him great credit with their Ford Cortinas and their cleanliness about the collar.

Am I right?

I am.

'Such smugness, Place. Such mediocrity. Awful.'

Mr Garlick stood in the foyer peering into the hall through the glass swing doors.

Next to him stood Hallam Place and Garfield, whom they had met coming out of the toilets by the biology lab.

Mr Garlick tugged at Garfield's sleeve.

'Such niceness, eh, Place Junior?' he said. 'Such overwhelming niceness.'

A hint of a blush came to Garfield's cheeks.

Mr Garlick chuckled and coughed and belched softly.

He peered through the doors again and said:

'I see your charming lady wife, Place Junior, is dancing with our friend, Fallows,' he said.

'Yes, sir,' said Garfield.

Then Mr Garfield put his mouth close to Hallam Place's ear and whispered:

'Such a magnificent bosom, she has. Take her home, my dear. Take her home.'

Before Hallam Place could reply, his mother pushed open the door and confronted them with a sniff of the nose and a flick of the shoulders.

'Hello, Mr Garlick,' she said. 'Do you remember me, Mr Garlick? I'm Mrs Place, Mr Garlick. I'm Hallam and Garfield's mother. My word, you're looking poorly. Isn't Mr

Garlick looking poorly, Garfield? Just look at his . . . Garfield!'

'Yes?' said Garfield.

'Your tie. You've got the knot loose. Come here this minute.'

She took hold of him and pulled him towards her roughly. Then she commenced to struggle with the knot of his tie.

He tried to draw himself away.

'Mother!' he said. 'Please.'

Mrs Place wrenched even more vigorously at his tie.

'Never mind "Mother. Please." You look an absolute rag riser dressed like that,' she said. 'It's an insult to your headmaster stood like this improperly dressed. He wasn't brought up to be improperly dressed, Mr Garlick. As soon as the elbows on his blazer began to wear out he was bought another quick at the Co-op haberdashery.

'Am I right?

'I am.'

She gave a final twitch to Garfield's tie and pushed him away.

'There,' she said. 'It's done. And think on – don't go fiddling with it again.'

She turned to Mr Garlick and smiled broadly.

'I'm sorry about our Hallam, Mr Garlick.'

'Sorry for what?' said Mr Garlick, glancing nervously at Hallam Place.

'Sorry for our Hallam's state of dress,' said Mrs Place. 'I told him when we came out. I said to him: "It's not clever being dressed like a rag and bone man, Hallam," I said. "You might think it's clever," I said. "But your friends won't. They won't be dressed like that. They'll be dressed in neat suits or navy blazer and flannels like Garfield," I said.'

Mr Garlick clicked his tongue and cocked his head to one side.

'But I rather like his dress,' he said. 'I think it's most

appropriate for a literary lion. Literary lions have the right to dress as they will. Who are we to pass judgement on their sartorial excesses or inadequacies?'

Mrs Place put her hands on her hips and looked him up and down silently.

And then she turned to Garfield and said in a crushingly loud stage whisper:

'What did I tell you? He's gone doodle alley pip. He's pots for rags.'

She smiled at Mr Garlick and addressed him as though she were talking to a backward child.

'Why don't you come into the hall, Mr Garlick? We're just setting up the running buffet, love. We've some smashing individual trifles in the running buffet. I bet you love trifles at your age, don't you?'

'For pete's sake, mother,' said Hallam Place.

'Don't you look at me in that tone of voice, Hallam,' his mother snapped. 'I know this is all a big joke for you. You've only come here to mock. You'll be writing it all up in your little notebook, won't you? And next thing we know we'll all be in one of your stories on the telly. Don't think I didn't recognize myself in that piece you did for the Two Ronnies. There's only one person you know who says: "Am I right? I am." And that person is me.

'Am I right?

'I am.'

She flicked her shoulders and sniffed sharply.

'Well, I've no time to be stood here megging. I've got the running buffet to supervise,' she said. She paused, looked Mr Garlick up and down, wafted a speck of dust off the lapels of his jacket and spoke to him slowly and distinctly. 'Right then, Mr Garlick. Into the hall you go, Mr Garlick. We've some lovely sandwiches waiting for you in the running buffet. They've got the crusts cut off so you'll be able to manage.

'Am I right?'
'I am.'

Into the hall we go.

They're laying out the running buffet in one of the alcoves.

Bossy ladies with bossy bosoms and butter beneath their fingernails.

Look at the dancers.

Do I recognize any of them?

Dyson.

Yes, that's Dyson all right. Hasn't changed a bit really. Weak chin. Apologetic ears.

Smile at Hazel.

She winks at me over the shoulder of J. A. Fallows.

Yes, she has got a magnificent bosom. Her legs are good, too. And her bum. Superb.

Does she bully Garfield? Does she humour him? Does she shake her head with sadness at him? Does she tap her feet with irritation?

Is she wretched?

Is she content?

Is she miserable or is she happy?

Is she . . .

Who's that waving at me?

Is it Parkin?

Bloody hell, it is, and he's as bald as a coot.

'Did I really produce all this dross, Place?' said Mr Garlick.

'All your own work,' said Hallam Place.

Mr Garlick moved closer to him and grasped him by the arm.

'Such ordinariness,' he said. 'Is there not a single convicted rapist present, my dear?'

'I doubt it.'

'No arsonists, no embezzlers, no soldiers of fortune, no barons of pornography?'

'No.'

Mr Garlick sighed.

'Such ordinariness,' he said. 'Such mediocrity.' He chuckled and clapped his hands behind his back.

'Superb, my dear,' he said. 'Superb.'

The record stopped. The dancers parted. And J. A. Fallows climbed on to the stage and addressed himself to the microphone.

'Your attention, please, ladies and gentlemen,' he said. 'Your attention, if you please.'

He smirked.

He preened himself.

'Ladies and gentlemen, I have now a most pleasant duty to perform,' he said. 'As you know, twenty-five years ago to this very day our boys grammar school and our girls grammar school joined forces to . . .'

'Get on with it.'

J. A. Fallows glared out at the throng of dancers.

There were titters and someone began to slow handclap.

J. A. Fallows raised his hand and continued:

'. . . as I was saying, twenty-five years ago to this very day the girls and boys out of our respective grammar schools joined forces to organize a dance which one and all deemed to be an outstanding success. With that in mind an organizing committee was formed earlier in the year to set in motion a function which would commemorate that earlier dance and afford an opportunity for all those who participated in . . .'

Suddenly Mr Garlick clutched hold of Hallam Place's arm.

'I can't bear this, Place,' he said. 'I have to go.'

He turned away and began to head towards the glass swing doors that led to the foyer.

J. A. Fallows, who had been watching him out of the corner of his eye during the course of his speech shouted out:

'No, don't go sir. Don't go. Ladies and gentlemen, may I introduce you to our guest of honour, our beloved former headmaster, Mr J. W. H. T. Garlick BA (Sheffield) MA (Bristol).'

He held up his hands and began to applaud.

The revellers turned to Mr Garlick and after a while joined J. A. Fallows in applauding.

Mr Garlick clutched Hallam Place's arm more tightly and pressed himself into him.

His smile was crooked. His eyes watered. He belched and he coughed.

Someone cheered.

Mr Garlick flinched and shuddered.

Someone shouted:

'Dance!'

Slowly at first and then enthusiastically the chant was taken up by the other revellers.

'Dance, dance, dance, dance, dance.'

Louder and louder grew the chants.

Chapter Eighteen

'Dance, dance, dance, dance.'

Twenty-five years ago they made the same chant.

Masses of sweating pubescent bodies.

Dull eyes. Dull mouths.

Future tennis club romeos, snug bar braggarts, golf club lechers, washers of Sunday morning cars, pushers of supermarket trolleys, drivers of mobile caravanettes, tenders of rows and rows and rows of suburban roses.

Even then trapped solid in mediocrity.

'Dance, dance, dance, dance.'

Detestable jerks.

Loathsome in their smugness.

Hideous in their insignificance.

'Dance, dance, dance, dance.'

And twenty-five years ago she did exactly the same as she's doing now.

Hazel stepped forward out of the throng and walked towards Mr Garlick.

She smiled at him and opened her arms to him.

'May I?' she said.

Mr Garlick cowered. She smiled. He coughed.

Then he said very softly:

'But I don't know how to dance.'

Hazel took hold of him and led him on to the dance floor.

Mr Ullapool placed a record on the gramophone and the music started.

Hazel smiled at him.

'It's easy,' she said. 'I'll show you.'

The dancers parted to allow them space in the centre of the dance floor.

'Slow, slow, quick, quick, slow,' said Hazel guiding him tenderly. 'It's easy, isn't it? It's not hard.'

A slow smile came to Mr Garlick's face.

'Twenty-five years ago,' he said softly. 'You did this twenty-five years ago.'

'That's right,' said Hazel. 'Just relax. Slow, slow, quick, quick, slow.'

Mr Garlick stared around him.

'Madame?' he said. 'Has anyone seen Madame?'

'Slow, slow, quick, quick, slow,' said Hazel, and she held him closer to her and smiled into his eyes.

'I haven't seen Madame all evening,' said Mr Garlick. 'Have you seen Madame?'

A plump pale-faced man in a navy blue blazer and blue and white hound's teeth trousers smiled at him and said:

'Nice to see you, sir. I'm Brearley. I always used to come second in geography.'

Hazel weaved her way through the crowded dance floor in the lee of the platform, where Mr Ullapool looked down and nodded his head and grinned.

'You all knew about Madame at the dance, didn't you?' said Mr Garlick. 'Everyone knew except me.'

'Relax,' said Hazel. 'Try and enjoy yourself.'

Mr Garlick nodded his head in acknowledgement of the greeting of a small, ginger-haired man dancing with an angular, dark-haired woman with a prominent nose.

'So you married your young man?' he said to Hazel.

'That's right,' said Hazel. 'Sway to the left – and turn. That's it.'

'And what of his brother?' said Mr Garlick.

'Slow, slow, quick, quick, slow. You're doing very well. You've got a natural rhythm.'

'You danced with him that night twenty-five years ago.'

'That's right.'

'Such a handsome boy he was,' said Mr Garlick. 'Such a talent he had. Such personality. And, my dear, the towering success he's achieved in life.'

He chuckled to himself.

'And yet you chose his brother for a partner,' he said.

'That's right,' said Hazel.

Mr Garlick chuckled again.

'Our great writer wrote it all wrong,' he said. 'He wrote the wrong end to the wrong scene.'

J. A. Fallows went to the microphone and announced that the buffet was about to be served.

Hazel turned to Mr Garlick and said:

'There are a great many other scenes my brother-in-law should have written, Mr Garlick.'

Well, I say it myself, but it's a lovely running buffet.

The sausage rolls are sticking, though.

I knew they would.

Rubbish.

But as for the table – it looks a treat.

We've sticks of celery in glass tumblers, all the sandwiches have got the crusts cut off, there's bowls of cheese dip and crisps and twiglets, we've got individual pork pies with a choice of picalilli or chutney, we've bridge rolls filled with boiled ham and tongue and brawn, we've a wonderful selection of jellies and trifles.

And as for the cakes.

Well, words fail me.

My ladies have excelled themselves on the fancies front.

They have.

Mrs Staham's coconut macaroons just melt in your mouth – literally.

And her jam sponge is tip top, too.

Just look at them all tucking in.

You'd wonder where they put it.

Am I right?

I am.

What a nice bunch of young people, too.

Mind you, I don't approve of that Mr Ullapool being here.

After what he did at the dance twenty-five years ago, I don't know what they were thinking of inviting him here.

And he's so shameless about everything, too.

I've seen him with my own eyes nodding and grinning at old man Garlick for all the world as though nothing had happened.

Mind you, I don't suppose Mr Garlick noticed.

I think he's doodle alley pip.

I do.

Look at him now.

He's sat there in a corner surrounded by people, and he's never stopped boozing.

He's gone through two bottles of red wine to my certain knowledge, and I've seen him filling up his hip flask.

He'll be addled, that's what it is.

Red wine does that to you.

Look at the French.

What a shower.

And all they do is guzzle red wine morning, noon and night.

Mr Garlick took another sip of wine.

'And you, Parkin, what are you doing with yourself now?' he said to the small man with ginger hair.

'Well, I've taken over the family butchers business, sir,' said Parkin.

'Splendid. Splendid.'

'We've got three shops now, and we're opening another on the new shopping precinct.'

'Bravo, my dear,' said Mr Garlick and he reached out and

touched Garfield on the arm. 'Place Junior. I wonder if it would be troubling you too much to ask for a spot more wine?'

'Not at all, sir,' said Garfield, and he poured out another glass of red wine.

Mr Garlick nodded his thanks and beamed at his companions.

'How splendid to see you all,' he said. 'Isn't that Cranston over there with that rather porcine young lady?'

'That's Greenhough, sir,' said J. A. Fallows. 'T. W. G. Greenhough. He's manager of the carpet department at the Co-op.'

'Dear Lord, how we have all prospered,' said Mr Garlick, and he giggled and took another long sip from his glass of wine.

'It must make you very proud, sir,' said J. A. Fallows.

'Positively bursting with pride, my dear Fallows,' said Mr Garlick. 'My cup runneth over.'

People began to move away from the buffet.

There was laughter and chatter.

The gold leaf on the honours board glowed. The sticky scents of stale perfume mingled with the acrid tang of after shave and festering socks.

'My word, isn't this fun?' said Mr Garlick, sitting back in his chair and spreading out his arms. 'All the chaps together, yarning about old times. All happy and contented with the success we've made of our lives. So comforting to me, my dears. And, of course, we all know about Place Senior here.'

'Oh yes,' said Dyson, stoop-shouldered and red-wristed. 'My wife's a great fan of your work.'

'Thank you,' said Hallam Place.

'And her mother.'

'Smashing.'

'And our next door neighbour.'

'And so they should be, Dyson,' said Mr Garlick. 'Place

Senior is the glittering megastar in the firmament of talent produced by this school. Am I not right, Place?'

Hallam Place smiled icily.

'Do you know lots of famous people then?' said Parkin.

'Famous people?' said Mr Garlick. 'My dear, Parkin, Place is on the most intimate terms with the most most famous people in the land. Am I not right, Place?'

Hallam Place stared at him hard, and not a flicker of emotion came to his face.

'Do you know Dick Emery?' said Parkin.

'Dick Emery! And the rest, my dear Parkin. And the rest,' said Mr Garlick, and he motioned for Garfield to refill his glass once more.

He drank deeply and smacked his lips.

'My dears,' he said. 'I really don't think you realize the stature your old chum holds in the community of those "who matter". His name is on "everyone's lips". His name is never out of the more "popular" newspapers – hobnobbing with the literary lions of London, dining with politicians, escorting glamorous film stars.'

He coughed and chuckled.

The lines at the corners of his eyes wrinkled.

Doris Day bumbled in the background. Plates clattered. The lights flickered.

Mr Garlick extended his arms to his audience.

'My dears, here is your chance to bask in the limelight of his fame,' he said. 'More than that. Ask him nicely, and who knows, he might rewrite your past, and he might rewrite your present and your future.'

Rewrite?

I looked at them at the dance twenty-five years ago, and already I was rewriting their future.

'What Will I Be In Twenty-Five Years Time.'

I watched them in their awkward collars and their stiff toecaps, and I rewrote their lives for them.

Hazel asked me to dance.

After a while she said:

'You can take me home if you want.'

And I said:

'What?'

And she said:

'Are you shy, Hallam? Are you frightened?'

And I said:

'No.'

And she said:

'You are. You're frightened.'

And I said:

'I'm thinking about Garfield. He's your boyfriend. What will he say?'

And I swear I heard Garlick say:

'Bugger, Garfield. Re-write the scene, boy. Re-write.'

I looked across at him.

He was on the other side of the hall, and he was smiling.

'Take me home,' said Hazel. 'I'm on my own in the house for the weekend. Mum and dad are away in the caravan at Prestatyn. You can stay the night.'

And I swear I heard Garlick's voice again, drumming into the deepest caverns of my brain.

'A neat little house on a neat little estate and rows and rows and rows of suburban roses.'

I looked over to him. His face was impassive.

'We can slip off now. No one will notice,' Hazel said, and she pressed herself into me and I felt the hard tip of her bra rasp against my shirt. 'I like you, Hallam. You can take my clothes off when we get home. I'll show you how to undo my bra. I'll let you look when I take my clothes off.'

'But what about Garfield?'

She hugged me. She gripped me tightly.

'Take me home, Hallam. Take me home,' she cried.

And, yes, I heard Garlick's voice say:

'And marry her, boy. Marry her.'

Mr Garlick continued to drink wine.

His face was flushed, his eyes sparkled and his laughter had a tinge of coarseness to it.

He watched Hallam Place dancing with Hazel, and he chuckled.

Mrs Place was standing next to Garfield. She, too, was watching the dancers.

'Isn't it lovely to see them dancing together, Garfield?'

'Yes,' said Garfield.

'I think it's nice how well your brother gets on with your wife, Garfield. That's what family life is all about.

'Am I right?

'I am.'

Garfield licked his lips dryly.

His brother danced with his wife.

His wife held his brother tightly in her arms.

'If only Hallam had married a girl like Hazel,' said Mrs Place. 'Eee, what a difference it would have made. He'd have had a neat little home, a neat little garden, a neat little life. What a difference it would have made.'

Hazel rested her head on Hallam Place's shoulder. She rubbed her thighs against him.

And Hallam Place heard, boring deep into his brain, the voice of Mr Garlick.

'What are your plans for her, Place? Tell me. Tell me. What a fine bosom she has. Such lovely long legs. Such flared nostrils. Tell me your plans for her.'

Hallam Place looked across to Mr Garlick.

He was slumped in his chair, and his mother was leaning over him, prodding him in the ribs with her forefinger.

'Mr Garlick?' she said. 'Mr Garlick, are you all right, Mr Garlick?'

Mr Garlick groaned.

He opened his eyes and said weakly:

'I'm a sick man, Mrs Place.'

'I know you are, love. That's what I told you before. You look right peeky to me.'

Hallam Place came to stand by her side.

He looked down on his old headmaster. Hazel held tightly to his hand, and Garfield hunched his shoulders.

'Madame!' said Mr Garlick. 'Where's Madame?'

Mrs Place glanced at Hallam Place and clicked her tongue.

'Now, now, Mr Garlick, you're not to go upsetting yourself like that,' she said. 'Have a maid of honour. There should be some left – they weren't very popular.'

Mr Garlick wiped his lips with the back of his hand.

'I remember so well the dance twenty-five years ago,' he said.

'Course you do, love,' said Mrs Place. 'The maids of honour didn't go then neither.'

'I was sitting on this very spot and I asked: "Where's Madame?" I was only talking to myself really. But your son, Hallam, was watching me. And he said: "Do you want to know where she is?" And I said: "Yes." Why did I say "Yes"?'

'I don't know, love, I'm sure,' said Mrs Place and once more she glanced at Hallam Place, but this time there was a look of deep concern on her face.

'Your son took me by the arm and he led me out through the hall doors and along the corridors. I knew what I would find. He took me to the sixth form room and he said: "Do you really want to go inside?" And I said: "Yes." Why did I say: "Yes"?'

'I don't know, love,' said Mrs Place.

'Your son flung open the door and switched on the lights.

And there they were. Madame and Ullapool. Her dress was undone to the waist and Ullapool was fondling her bosom with his wet clammy hands. And . . . And . . .'

And you did nothing, you old fraud.

You stood there, and the corners of your eyes crinkled.

And you said nothing as Madame stood up and dusted down her dress.

And you did nothing as Ullapool barged past you and fled down the corridor.

And you did nothing as Madame pushed past you, her head held high, her eyes gleaming, her great booming breasts still uncovered.

And after a while you turned to me and said:

'I don't suppose you could re-write that, could you, Place?'

Yes, my son, I could.

I could re-write anything you want.

I could re-write a suitable ending for you.

J. A. Fallows stepped on to the platform once more to the accompaniment of derisive jeers and slow handclaps.

He blew into the microphone, tapped it with his middle fingers and then spoke.

'I wonder, ladies and gentlemen, if you would gather round the platform in front of me as we approach the highspot of our evening's jollifications.'

The dancers collected reluctantly round the platform. Their faces were flushed. Their stockings were wrinkled. Their collars were damp.

J. A. Fallows looked down on them and beamed with deep contentment.

He raised his hand.

'Ladies and gentlemen, the time has now come for us to turn our attentions to our beloved and revered former headmaster. Mr Garlick, I wonder if you would kindly step on stage to receive our presentation?'

'Presentation?' said Mr Garlick. 'What have you hatched up for me?'

Hallam Place took hold of him by the elbow and raised him to his feet.

'Come on, my dear. On to the stage with you,' he said.

He led him towards the stage.

Mr Garlick made no resistance.

'Don't worry, my dear,' said Hallam Place. 'I'll stick very close to you.'

J. A. Fallows led the applause enthusiastically as Hallam Place led Mr Garlick on to the stage.

The old headmaster stood next to J. A. Fallows blinking and rubbing the palms of his hands on the side of his trousers.

J. A. Fallows held up his hand to stop the applause.

Then he spoke at the microphone once more.

'Ladies and gentlemen, most of you will be cognizant of the fact that I was head boy of our grammar school during what I like to call "its halcyon days".

'Our rugby team, undefeated for three successive seasons, contained several men who were later to achieve county honours at senior level. In athletics our high hurdlers were feared the length and breadth of the district. And so were our thespian colleagues in the field of amateur dramatics.

'But now, ladies and gentleman, the end of an era is nigh.

'As you know, at the end of this term this school will cease to be a grammar school.

'As from September next it will become a comprehensive school.

'Now far be it from me to indulge in matters of a political nature. All I will say is that for the legions of young men who passed through this grammar school there will be nothing but sadness and despair.

'However, Mr Garlick, sir, your efforts have not been in vain.

'You see before you the products of those who have been at the grammar.

'Look at them, sir, and there you will see your true memorial.'

The dancers applauded.

Mr Garlick shielded his eyes with the flat of his hand and peered out on to the dance floor.

He began to tremble.

J. A. Fallows stopped the applause and resumed his speech.

'In order, sir, to show our appreciation we wish to make this presentation to you.'

'Presentation?' said Mr Garlick. 'What are you doing to me, Place?'

'Hush,' said Hallam Place. 'Listen to Fallows.'

'Our presentation to you, sir, takes the form of a portrait. And you will be pleased to know that it has been painted by one of your ex-pupils, T. H. B. T. Tattersall.'

'Young Tattersall?'

'That's right,' said Hallam Place.

J. A. Fallows turned to the wings of the stage.

'Tattersall, if you please,' he said.

To the applause of the dancers Tattersall stepped on to the stage. He carried a painting under his arm.

He stood in front of Mr Garlick.

'Mr Garlick, on behalf of everyone connected with the school I should like to . . .'

'Place, Place,' whispered Mr Garlick. 'Why is he wearing school uniform? Why hasn't he aged like the rest of you?'

'Hush,' said Hallam Place. 'Listen.'

'. . . the great affection and appreciation we have for you, sir,' continued Tattersall.

'He hasn't aged,' whispered Mr Garlick. 'He's the same as he was that day I caught him in the urinals.'

'. . . and so on behalf of all your admirers, Mr Garlick, I should like to present you with this portrait I have painted. It is a painting of Madame.'

'Madame?' said Mr Garlick, and he clutched at his throat and began to reel backwards.

Hallam Place held him steady.

'Hush,' he said. 'Listen.'

Tattersall stepped forward and handed the painting to Mr Garlick.

He pulled back the protective sheets.

And he saw a painting of Madame.

She was completely naked lying on her back.

And on her firm booming breasts were the clammy hands of Mr Ullapool.

Mr Garlick gasped and then he collapsed to the ground.

The dancers applauded.

Chapter Nineteen

Isn't it tragic when someone goes and dies like that?

It's such a waste.

It was exactly the same with the milkman's horse.

Keeled over in the street last Whit Monday and in the knacker's yard by the Tuesday.

Poor soul.

He was a lovely horse, was Armageddon.

He was very fond of shredded wheat.

He liked Taverner's fruit drops, too, particularly the green ones.

And talking about horses and boiled sweets, have you been able to buy a tin of Zubes lately?

I haven't.

I don't think you can whack a good Zube when you're feeling throaty.

'Hoarse? Go Suck A Zube.' – my word, there were never truer words spoken.

Am I right?

I am.

Now where was I?

Ah, yes, Mr Garlick.

Poor devil dying like that.

I went with him in the ambulance to hospital and all he did was mumble.

I couldn't make head nor tail of it.

'Speak up, love, if you want me to understand,' I kept saying to him. 'Open your mouth and take deep breaths.'

But no.

All he did was mumble on about Tattersall being dressed

in school uniform and the picture of Madame being in the nude.

What a load of nonsense.

Tattersall was wearing a beautiful suede jacket with cavalry twill trousers and a blue cashmere sweater.

He looked a treat.

Not like our Hallam.

And as for the picture of Madame; it was respectability personified.

I never saw her look so respectable in real life.

I did not.

It would have been truer to life if she had been painted in her birthday suit.

Well, she was never backwards in coming forwards when it came to showing her do-dahs.

Isn't it rude, when women do things like that?

Poor old Garlick.

I think it's the drink that did for him.

You should have seen him at the dance. Glass after glass after glass of red wine. His face was as flushed as a boiled beetroot, his eyes were bloodshot and his hands never stopped trembling.

Booze.

That was his downfall, and I don't intend to say another word on the subject.

As far as I'm concerned it is a closed book.

Mind you, he did have a lovely turn-out for the funeral.

You should have seen the floral tributes.

And thank goodness Hallam didn't let me down neither.

Much to my amazement he went out and bought himself a decent suit. I couldn't get him to wear a tie, though. It defies all credence, doesn't it? He goes and buys himself a brand new suit, and then he won't go and wear a tie with it.

It's sheer stubbornness, is that.

Mind you, stubbornness runs in the family.

You take Avril, for example.

Now you'll have noticed that she's my only daughter, and I haven't mentioned her so far.

The reason is simple – I am thoroughly ashamed of her.

She got herself into a mess.

And do you know why – sheer stubbornness.

Why she had to go and marry that Vernon Hemingway when she could have had half a dozen like Geoffrey Lancaster is totally and completely and utterly beyond me.

I'm not saying anything personal against Vernon.

He was a nice enough little fellow if you ignored the big lobes to his ears.

It was his background that stuck in my gullet.

I'm not being snobbish, but he was so working class and Avril just wasn't brought up to those sort of standards.

We're middle class and proud of it.

We've always had fitted carpets and soft toilet paper. We've never once had our phone cut off. We always watch BBC in preference to ITV.

And to think Avril threw that all away to marry a common or garden working class storeman in a furniture repository who's never once set eyes on a satsuma till he came to our house that Christmas.

No wonder she had a gifted child.

It was a punishment for her.

No wonder she made such a mess of things.

I'll tell you what happened.

Chapter Twenty

Things started to go really wrong about two years after Curtis was born.

He's the child they had, is Curtis.

I remember going to visit Avril.

Oh, she did live in a poor little neighbourhood.

They tried to keep it nice, mind you, but they were fighting a losing battle what with the ropeworks and the heavy lorries and the damp from the canal.

It was a terraced house she lived in with a back entry and an outside toilet.

It always looked so pinched and hangdog from the outside. It always looked guilty.

I felt ashamed taking the taxi driver there.

Well, that sort of thing can go against you, you know. They put it around, do taxi drivers, and I've got a very good reputation amongst the proprietors of hackney carriages in this town.

Anyway, I told him to come back for me in an hour's time and to make sure he emptied his ashtrays in the meantime.

It was one of those houses where the front door was always open. You didn't have to knock to go in.

And that's another thing that stuck in my gullet.

It's so working class to keep your front door off the latch.

A front door's for keeping people out not to let them in.

Am I right?

I am.

If there's one thing I cannot abide it's people who pop in unexpectedly.

'We were just passing, Nerys, so we thought we'd pop in and see how you are,' they say.

You know what my answer is?

On your bike.

That's what I say.

On your bike.

And I can't stand eating a meal with people sat on the sofa watching me.

That's working class, too.

And those are the sort of habits Avril had got into that day I visited her.

I walked straight in and I was greeted by that working class smell.

You know what I mean?

It's quite distinctive from a nice middle class smell.

It's a mixture of cheap cooking and damp mufflers. It's a mixture of bad chests and old mongrels and night lights and cold bedrooms and wet batteries and dolly blues and soot and laziness.

It's not a nice smell like a nice middle class smell, is it?

Anyway it was very much in evidence when I walked into Avril's back parlour.

Back Parlour?

What a disgusting expression.

She wasn't brought up to use words like that, I can tell you.

It was dining room at the back and lounge at the front.

Back Parlour!

Disgusting.

No wonder she let herself go.

She was sitting at the table when I walked in and the dirty pots hadn't even been sided from breakfast.

There were cinders in the grate and clothes flung any old how over the clothes horse and . . .

Oh, it made my blood boil, I can tell you.

'Just look at the state of this, Avril,' I said. 'You were never brought up to run a home like this. Am I right? I am.'

And she said in a weak little voice without looking up:

'Mother.'

'It's a shambles,' I said. 'It's a disgrace. When I think of the way I brought you up, it makes my blood boil. Literally. You had a lovely taste in soft furnishings when you were a teenager, and look at this lot – Rubbish.'

'Mother, please,' she said.

'Never mind "mother please",' I said. 'I warned you this would happen. Marrying beneath yourself into the working classes was tantamount to treachery.'

'Mother,' she said, and she looked up and her hair was all straggly and there were nicotine stains on her fingernails.

'To think a daughter of mine can only afford to travel by train on Persil vouchers. Disgusting,' I said, and I meant it, too. 'There were scores of young men lining up to marry you. You could have had your pick. Look at Geoffrey Lancaster. He was daft about you, was Geoffrey Lancaster. If you'd married Geoffrey Lancaster, you'd have been living in the lap of luxury. Continental holidays abroad. Automatic Volvos changed every year. Cashmere cardies whenever you wanted. If you'd married Geoffrey Lancaster . . .'

'Bugger, Geoffrey Lancaster,' she said. 'Bugger him.'

The language. Honestly.

She was never brought up to use language like that.

Flipping heck was as much as she said in the days when she was middle class.

I looked at her long and hard, and I said:

'Are you feeling poorly, Avril?'

'No,' she said. 'I'm feeling fine.'

'Well, you don't look it to me,' I said. 'You haven't looked right for weeks. There's something worrying you, isn't there?'

'Yes,' she said.

'It's money, isn't it?' I said. 'Well, that's what comes of marrying beneath your class. I know Vernon's a nice little man in his own way, but . . .'

'It's not money, mother.'

'Well, what is it then?'

'Our Curtis.'

Oooh, I felt a dagger go through my heart, when she said that.

I mean, I know I'm not very keen on young children what with their messy eating habits and their sticky out ears, but, when all's said and done, Curtis is flesh and blood, isn't he?

'He's not been taken poorly, has he, Avril?' I said.

'No, mother,' she said. 'He's started reading the newspaper.'

'At two years of age?' I said.

'Yes,' she said. 'Every day he reads *The Evening Telegraph and Argus* from cover to cover. Births, Marriages and Deaths. Stop press racing results. Percy Thrower's Gardening Hints.'

'At two years of age?' I said.

I mean, I could hardly believe my ears.

'Yes,' said Avril. 'At two years of age.'

Oh dear.

Oh dear, oh dear.

I knew instantly we were heading for trouble.

Chapter Twenty-one

Hullo, folks.

It's me.

Curtis.

How are you diddling?

I see James Cameron wrote another load of old shite in *The Guardian* this morning.

I hear things I didn't ought to hear.

I'm only two, yet the things they say in front of me. Take me dad and his mate, Sam.

We're sitting outside this pub, The Bargeman's Comfort.

It's on the banks of the canal and it's not bad really.

You can see the grooves in the tow path made by the horses' hooves, and there are iron rings where they moored their barges.

Sam and me old man are sitting on a wall supping their pints and talking.

And I hear things I didn't ought to hear.

'You see, Sam, Curtis is only two years of age. He's two, Sam. That is the total sum of his lifespan thus far.'

'Mm.'

'And two is a funny age to be asking your father what the capital of Afghanistan is.'

'Mm.'

'I come home from the furniture repository last night, Sam, and he's sat in his chair, is our Curtis, engrossed in *The New Statesman* and *Nation*, and he looks up at me and he says: "Dad," he says. "What's the capital of Afghanistan?"'

'At two years of age?'

'Correct, Sam. Spot on.'

'What's he want to know that for?'

'No, Sam, no, you've got it wrong. He knows what the capital of Afghanistan is, does Curtis. It's me what's in the dark as regards that, Sam. Total dark.'

Their lips sluck at their beer.

A swan spins in an eddy of the wind.

And once more I hear things I didn't ought to hear.

I'm in the back parlour now.

My mother talks to my father.

'He's done what, Avril?'

'He's written a letter to the editor of *The Guardian*.'

'At two years of age?'

'Yes.'

'What's he wrote about then?'

'Nancy Banks Smith.'

'What's that?'

'I don't know. Eee, it's weird is all this, isn't it, Vernon?'

'Mm.'

'He's only two years of age, Vernon. He's far too young to be writing letters to the editor of *The Guardian*.'

'Mm.'

'Mm.'

'Oh, Vernon, what are we going to do?'

'Search me, Avril. What's for supper?'

'Haslet, pigs' trotters and brown bread and butter.'

Munch munch.

Munch munch.

I remember the day I was born.

Squalls from the north west. Canal furrowed. Bleak gulls on bleak winter parks.

The midwife held me in her arms.

'It's a boy, Mrs Hemingway,' she said. 'You've given birth to a boy.'

'Thank you,' said my mother. 'Is it all right? Is it all in one piece?'

I remember it so well.

The midwife bunged me in a cot at the side of my mother's bed.

I lay there quite still, quite silent, listening.

Scutter of sparrows in gutter. Chatter of tea cups. Patter of nurses' footsteps.

Father came to visit mother.

He had a bunch of flowers.

'I've brought you these,' he said.

'Thank you.'

'They're flowers.'

'I know,' said mother. 'They're very nice.'

He stood there, shuffling his feet and fiddling with his thumbs.

'Do you want to see him then?' said mother.

'Who?' he said.

'Our baby.'

'Oh yes. Ta very much then. Is this him then?'

'Yes.'

'I see.'

'What do you think of him then, Vernon?'

He bent over my cot.

Sag of mouth. Dull eyes. Razor scars on scrawny neck. Damp. Totally damp.

'Well?' said my mother after a while. 'What do you think?'

'His eyes are funny, aren't they?' said my father.

'How do you mean?'

'The way he looks at you.'

'How do you mean, Vernon?'

'He looks at you as though he knows something we don't. Something really important.'

Sure do, buddy.

Ah surely does.

They brought me home.

One evening my mother's mother came round in a taxi.

And I heard things I didn't ought to have heard.

'He's an ugly little devil, isn't he?' said Mrs Place.

'What?' said my mother.

'Oh, I'm not being disparaging about you, Avril. You couldn't help it. It's the working class sperms you've got to blame.'

'Mother! I wish you'd give it a rest.'

She bent over my pram.

Flakes of powder fell from her nose. She had lipstick on her two front teeth.

She prodded me.

'He's not like other babies, is he, Avril? Be rights he should be all chubby and pink and smelling of milk. But him . . . well, it's as though there was an adult staring at you out of that pram.'

My mother began to sob.

She sank down in the armchair and her mother went up to her and put her hand tentatively on her shoulder.

'There, there, Avril, love,' she said.

My mother sniffled into her handkerchief.

'I'm so worried about Curtis,' she said. 'He's only six weeks old, mother, yet he lies in his pram in the back parlour every evening, and it's as though he's listening to every word Vernon and I say. It's as though he can understand every word. And he has this look on his face as though we were talking utter rubbish. He's criticizing us, pulling us to pieces, looking at us with utter contempt.'

Mrs Place (I can't bear to call her grannie or nana) stroked my mother's cheek.

'There, there, Avril,' she said. 'Don't upset yourself, love. You're reading things into his ugly little face which aren't there. Babies don't understand us adults, love. Babies don't understand anything.'

I do.

I understand everything.

Outside every child there's an adult screaming to get in. Kicking and screaming. Scratching and clawing to escape from the body of the adult into the body of the child.

No one ever makes it.

I did.

Oh yes, folks, I did.

Chapter Twenty-two

The years passed and things got worse.

At the age of two-and-a-half he started reading H. E. Bates and by the time he was three he was contradicting them on 'Round Britain Quiz'.

His mother just couldn't cope.

It was a relief when they let him start school at four years of age.

I remember so well watching him set off with his mother that first day at school.

I'll say it myself, but he did look a picture with his little cherry red cap and his *Financial Times* rolled up under his arm.

My first day at school.

Widdle, wail and whimper. Scratch and bite.

Not me folks.

Cool and calm, yours truly.

In control.

Playtime.

A knee-chapped yard. Tumble of milk-sour bodies. Widdle, wail and whimper. Scratch and bite.

Not me, folks.

I stood aloof.

Cold.

Calm.

Then this little girl came over.

Oh Christ.

'Hello, little boy,' she said.

What a pain in the backside, eh?

'My name's Elisabeth. Do you want to be my friend? You can be my friend, if you like. Would you like to be my friend?'

Shove off sweetheart.

Leave me alone.

'You're shy. I'll look after you, if you like. Would you like me to look after you? I won't let the big kids hit you. If you be my friend, I'll look after you, little boy. Would you like me to look after you?'

Go away.

Piss off.

'My dad's a fitter at Baldwin-Hardcastles. What is your dad, little boy?'

My dad?

Little girl, my dad's a baby.

My dad?

He's all right, is my dad.

He's a bit thick.

He's not got much upstairs.

But he's all right.

It was nice when he took me to the furniture repository.

Gentle gloom. Cool.

Desks. Wardrobes. Tables. Sofas, armchairs, brooding double beds.

Silent.

Still.

Just like a school of stranded whales.

And my dad talked so proudly about me to his boss, Mr Pawson.

Nice man, Mr Pawson.

Got a big conk.

'He's took to school like a duck takes to water, has our Curtis, Mr Pawson.'

'Has he now, Vernon? Has he be God?'

'Yes, Mr Pawson. He comes home from school, does our

Curtis, Mr Pawson, and he's full of it. Well, for him he is. You see, Mr Pawson, he doesn't say much, doesn't our Curtis. Which is very strange in a way.'

'And why's that, Vernon?'

'Well, you see, Mr Pawson, thinking doesn't run in our family.'

'No?'

'No. We don't go in for things like that in our family. We've no history of it.'

'It's a great gift, is thinking, when you come to think about it, Vernon.'

'It is that, Mr Pawson. I wonder who gave the gift to our Curtis?'

I know.

I know who gave me the gift.

Hallam.

He's the writer.

He's the one who doles out the largesse.

Wow, the plot thickens, eh?

Stick close to me, and I'll reveal more.

I hear things I didn't ought to hear.

I wasn't there, but I heard everything that happened when my headmistress, Mrs Mazarene, called my mother and father to see her at school.

Nice lady, Mrs Mazarene.

Blue grey hair severely cut. Splayed feet. Prominent jaw line. I think she could have been a bit of a raver, when she was younger.

She met my mother and father in her study.

Nice study.

Overlooked the school garden.

She told them to sit down, and then she said:

'I've asked you both to come and see me, because I want to

talk to you about Curtis.'

'Oh dear,' said my mother. 'He's not been causing trouble, has he, Mrs Mazarene?'

'Oh no, Mrs Hemingway, quite the reverse. Curtis is a jewel. Curtis is a diamond who glitters and sparkles.'

'I beg your pardon?' said my mother.

'I am trying to tell you, Mrs Hemingway, that Curtis is what we in educational circles term "a gifted child".'

My mother looked at my father.

He turned his eyes away from her.

'I'm sorry, Mrs Mazarene, I don't understand,' she said.

'I'll explain. To put it quite simply, Mrs Hemingway, your son, Curtis, has the highest intelligence quotient of any child who has attended this school in the whole thirty-seven years of its history.'

'Oh heck,' said my father. 'I'm right sorry about that.'

'I beg your pardon?' said Mrs Mazarene.

'Well, if me and his mum had known that, we'd have knocked it out of him sharpish, wouldn't we, Avril?'

Lovely Mrs Mazarene.

Pearl grey twin set and sensible brogues.

She smiled at my father.

Snow white teeth.

Smooth, firm neck.

'Mr Hemingway,' she said gently. 'I don't think you quite understand the significance of what I am telling you. Your son is way way above average intelligence. In all my career as a teacher I have never met a child of such natural outstanding academic brilliance.

'Mr Hemingway, Curtis is a genius.

'Mr Hemingway, your son is a truly gifted child.'

Gifted child!

What a load of old rubbish.

Am I right?

I am.

I know his uncles were always clever at the grammar school.

I mean, Hallam always came top or thereabouts in English.

And Garfield, when he put his mind to it, always cut a fine dash in difficult sums.

But there was never any question whatsoever of them being gifted.

They don't allow that sort of thing when you belong to the middle class.

That was the whole point of my argument when I went by taxi to see Avril.

'A gifted child, Avril?' I said. 'I've never heard such rubbish in the whole of my life.'

'But his headmistress told us personally, mother. She told us face to face, didn't she, Vernon?'

Well, I wasn't going to let him get his two pennorth in.

What does he know about it?

He's only the father.

'What does Mrs Mazarene know about it?' I said. 'She's only the headmistress. She's just trying to blind you with science, that's all. She's just making excuses.'

'What excuses?' said Avril.

My Lord, she can be so stupid, when she puts her mind to it, can Avril.

'Excuses for Curtis not being like other children,' I said. 'At his age he should be out in the street swinging round lamp posts and chasing cats. He's far too young to be reading Pears Encyclopaedia. No wonder his cap doesn't fit him.'

'Why?'

'Because his head is far too big for his age. And why? Because his head is stuffed full of stuff he's no business knowing at his age. What he needs is a thorough good sharacking. And he should have been breast fed, too. I told you at the time. No wonder his underpants are always falling down round his ankles.'

'Why?'

'Because, Avril, because he's not got the constitution to hold them up. A gifted child! What a load of old rubbish.'

Chapter Twenty-three

My seventh birthday.

Presents.

From my mother and from my father – a football.

From my mother's mother – shin pads.

From Mrs Mazarene – three Arthur Ransome books.

Wonderful.

John and Susan, Roger and Kitty, Dick and Dorothea, Nancy and Peggy.

Whatever became of them when they grew up?

John?

Torpedoed in the war on a frigate in the China Sea.

'Make sure the chaps are safe, Number One.

'Swallows and Amazons for ever.'

Nancy?

Tweeds, thick brogues and a black moustache.

And Peggy?

Poor old Peggy.

A gin-sodden hulk in a London bed-sit.

Marriage destroyed.

Only Roger to see her now and then with a grin and a bottle of gin.

Poor, poor Peggy.

You should have married me.

Hey ho.

If only, if only.

If only they hadn't given me a birthday party.

What a drag.

Little boys and little girls in funny hats.

Parents in their Sunday best.

Mother's mother powdered and painted.

And Elisabeth.

Oh God, she had to come over to me of course.

A prize mitherer, Elisabeth.

'I don't like your party,' she said. 'I think your party's rubbish.'

How very interesting.

'And so do Beryl Ritchings and Winifred Duffin.'

Arseholes to Beryl Ritchings and Winifred Duffin.

'We had a conjuror at my party.'

So?

'He was a real conjuror, too.'

Big deal.

She stuck out her tongue and they started to play musical chairs.

My mother chivvied my father, and her mother said:

'He's rubbish, Avril. Total rubbish. If only you'd married Geoffrey Lancaster. Dear oh dear. If you'd married Geoffrey Lancaster, you'd have been in clover now.

'Am I right?

'I am.'

I settled myself in a corner of the room and began to read one of my new books.

Arthur Ransome.

The house boat on the frozen winter lake. Mumps. Peggy. I love you, Peggy. You should have married me, Peggy.

Bloody hell, what a life I have to offer you.

I'm trapped, Peggy.

Just like the houseboat on the frozen lake.

No escape.

I glanced across, and there he was, reading books at his own birthday party.

It's not natural.

'It's not natural, Avril,' I said. 'He's always reading

books. Hallam and Garfield were always reading books, I grant you.

'But only in context, Avril.

'Only in context.

'That's the way to read books – in context.'

They all went home.

I went to bed.

Tick of clock.

Tock of clock.

Cold rasp of my bedroom's breath.

The door creaked open.

'Curtis? Curtis, it's your dad. Are you asleep, Curtis?'

Clench my eyelids tightly shut.

Clench my fists.

Breathe soft and deep.

'They've gone, Curtis. They've all gone home.'

I know, you berk.

'Your mum's right upset with you, Curtis. And she's cross with me. She's just given me a terrible sharacking. Terrible.'

Oh, God, he's getting into bed with me.

He's lying alongside me.

'When I was little like you, Curtis, I used to go to Liverpool for me summer holidays. I stayed with Uncle Harmer. The first two nights I used to lie in bed sobbing my heart out. And Uncle Harmer would come upstairs and he'd lie down on the bed like what I'm doing now, and he'd talk to me like what I'm talking to you now.'

Don't respond.

Don't encourage him.

Don't let on you're awake.

'He was a steward with the Isle of Man Steam Packet Co., was me Uncle Harmer. And he'd tell me all about the ships he'd sailed on.

'*Mona's Isle*.

'*Manx Maid*.

'*Ben Ma Chree*.

'Nice names, eh?

'And he'd tell me about the rough seas and drinking cocoa with the cooks in the galley. And he'd talk about Liverpool and what it was like when he was a little lad. He used to go to a chippie where they cooked on a coke-fired stove. He used to walk with his dad under the Docker's Umbrella. He used to run barefoot on the Cast Iron shore.

'And I could visualize it all, Curtis.

'I could see it right clearly.

'I could see the sea heaving. I could smell the smoke from the coke fire. I could hear the waves rippling on the Cast Iron shore.

'And I never did nothing about it in later life.

'And now I can't visualize nothing.

'Don't grow up to be like me, Curtis.

'Take a tip from your dad.'

Tick of clock.

Tock of clock.

Cold rasp of bedroom's breath.

'I like looking at you, Curtis, when you're fast asleep.

'I wish I could curl up inside you.

'Deep inside you, Curtis.

'Right down deep inside you.'

I hear things I didn't ought to hear.

The back parlour.

My father sits at the table working on his model battleship.

Mother sides the pots.

'Mother says we've got to take action,' she said.

'Mm.'

'She says we've got to do something about him.'

'Why?'

'Because he's not normal. You heard what Mrs Mazarene said. He's a gifted child. Well, we can't have that, Vernon. Mother says it's making me a laughing stock in the dry cleaner's.'

'Mm.'

'Look what happened in Tesco's last Friday. Do you know what he said?'

'No.'

'Well, I was just reaching up to get a tin of greengage and apple pie filling and he said: "Mum, do giraffes procreate like what we do?" Well! I gave him such a clout. Imagine it, Vernon – procreation in Tesco's.'

'Aye, it is a bit rum, is that.'

'You've got to do something about it. Don't leave it all to me. I can't cope on my own.'

Next day he took me to the furniture repository.

It was cool.

It was gloomy.

'Do you like it here, Curtis?'

Course I do, you barmy berk.

'I do. I like the smell of the wood. I like the way it glows. Good wood always glows, Curtis.'

'Mm.'

'I like to touch it. I like to rub my hands over it. Lancewood. Maple, oak and pine. Rosewood. Yew, tupelow and ebony that croons.'

'Mm.'

'Mahogany. That's the best wood of all to touch, Curtis. It yields to your touch. It responds to it. I've heard tell that women do that sometimes.'

And then he did a most peculiar thing.

He crouched down. He took the legs of the mahogany taboret in his hands. And he stroked them. Very softly. With a long, slow smile on his face.

I could do something for you.

Oh aye.

Somewhere deep inside you, father, there's a gifted adult striving to get out.

I hear things I didn't ought to hear.

The back parlour and my mother and her mother eating.

'Rows, rows, rows, that's all Vernon and I have all day long,' said my mother.

'Fancy.'

'He was always so kind and so calm, was Vernon. He wouldn't say boo to a goose.'

'I know, Avril. He's never been the same since Curtis was born. Right from the moment of his birth he never showed the slightest concern about his affliction.'

'What affliction, mother?'

'Being a gifted child, Avril. Never mind the shame it's brought on us. It doesn't seem to bother him that I'd be sat on the top deck of the 13B bus with my own grandson and heir, aged three and a half, reading "Confessions of an English Opium Eater."'

'I know, mother, I know. And all those questions. Questions, questions, questions. From the moment Curtis gets up to the moment he goes to bed all we get from him is questions, questions, questions. What's the capital of Italy? What's the capital of Denmark? What's the capital of Oslo? On and on and on.'

'Well, as I always say, Avril – men are buggers for geography.'

'Do you know, mother, I think Vernon's proud of him, if the truth be known.'

'Oh dear, oh dear, Avril. The scandal of it.'

My father lay in a piping hot bath.

His model battleship floated on the surface of the soap-pocked water.

I kneeled at the side of the bath and said:

'Come on. Try again. The capital of Afghanistan is . . . is . . . is . . . Come on, father. Think.'

And he screwed up his face and said:

'Kashmir.'

And I said:

'No. No, no, no. Kashmir's a province of India. Summer capital – Srinagar. Winter capital – Jammu.'

'I don't know, Curtis lad. I don't know.'

'You do. I told you yesterday.'

'I know you did. That's the whole trouble. I've forgot. I've not got the head for remembering things, Curtis.'

'You have, you have, you have. Now think. Think, think, think.'

'I can't. Oh, Curtis lad, what am I going to do?'

I hear things I didn't ought to hear.

Downstairs in the back parlour mother and her mother jabbered.

Father steamed slowly in the bath.

His battleship listed to port.

On and on and on they jabbered.

'You see, mother, Curtis is breaking up our marriage.'

'Well, if that's the case, Avril, you'll have to do something about it.'

'But what, mother?'

'Put him in a home.'

'A home?'

'It'll be a kindness to him, Avril. He'll be among his own kind. They have special homes for people who are good at multiplication tables.'

'Oh yes?'

'Of course they have. He'll be able to sit in the home, multiplying away to his heart's content.'

'Poor little thing.'

'They'll have colour telly, you know.'

'Will they?'

'Oh yes. They'll have several so you'll have a choice of channels and there'll be no battling over the knobs when he wants to watch Mastermind.'

Father raised himself from the bath.

The water cascaded off him.

It poured from his sharp elbows and made runnels down the insides of his thin little legs.

'On and on and on they go, Curtis,' he said.

'Correct.'

'All my married life your mother and her mother have jabbered at each other. On and on. On and on and on.'

'Correct.'

'I had dreams, you know. When I sat silent in the chair in the back parlour, my head wasn't empty like her and mother thought. It was full of dreams, Curtis. Full of thoughts. Full of wonderment. I wonder how the wireless works. Why does your skin go wrinkled if you stay in the bath too long?'

'What's the capital of Afghanistan?'

'I don't know.'

'You do. Think. Use your brain.'

'The capital of Afghanistan is . . . is . . . is Kabul.'

'Correct. What is the most desirable attribute in your wife?'

'Pass.'

'What attracted you to her in the first place?'

'Pass.'

'Are you happy with her?'

'Pass.'

'Answer.'

'Pass, Curtis. Pass, pass, pass.'

Chapter Twenty-four

If only she'd married Geoffrey Lancaster.

I mean, I know he's not much to look at physically, poor devil, but he has got security.

What security has meladdo got to give her?

A storeman in a furniture repository?

Where's the future in that?

You don't go on continental holidays to the continent on the sort of money he'll be earning.

You don't have fitted carpets and built-in wardrobes and en suite bathrooms.

You don't have a holiday cottage in North Wales in a village whose name you can't pronounce.

You don't have all the refinements of life like integral pelmets and special clippers for your toenails.

All you get is trouble.

And a gifted child.

Mrs Mazarene asked my mother and father to call in and see her.

I went with them and sat in a corner of the headmistress's study.

She had flowers on her desk.

'I've asked you both to come and see me because I'm worried about Curtis,' she said.

'I see,' said my mother.

'His academic record is brilliant. Superb. As you both know he is a gifted child. But what worries me, Mrs Hemingway, is his social attitude.'

'I don't quite follow you, Mrs Mazarene,' said my mother.

Mrs Mazarene tapped on her desk top with the tip of her silver propelling pencil.

'To put it bluntly, Mrs Hemingway, Curtis is anti-social.'

'Oh.'

'His relationship to his peers is poor. He refuses to communicate with them. His social adaptability is gravely deficient. His involvement in the welfare and interests of others is non-existent. Do you follow me, Mrs Hemingway?'

'I'm not quite sure, Mrs Mazarene.'

'Well, let me put it another way, Mrs Hemingway. Has Curtis got any friends at home?'

'Well, now you come to say that, Mrs Mazarene, I don't think he has. Has he got any friends at home, Vernon?'

'Yes,' said my father.

'Who?' said my mother.

'Me,' said my father.

And so we went for a walk, father and me.

We walked along the canal tow path, and then we cut through the brick works and into the meadows and down to the river.

We sat on the bank.

A bird was singing.

'Beautiful that,' said my father. 'What is it, Curtis?'

'A willow warbler.'

'Willow warbler. Beautiful name is that, isn't it, Curtis?'

'Beautiful.'

He shook his head with slow pleasure. He breathed in deeply. He closed his eyes.

'How did you know it was a willow warbler, Curtis?' he said.

'From books,' I said. 'You can learn a lot from books. Books open your eyes to things.'

'Do they?'

'Oh aye,' I said. 'Books give you release. Books take you into new worlds.'

He opened his eyes and stared at me.

Then he said softly:

'I could do with that, Curtis. I don't reckon much to the world I'm in now.'

'I know.'

He shook his head again. But this time it was with sadness.

'When I was young, I thought the perfect woman would be the Sunday roast of my life,' he said. 'Succulent. Rare. Rich juices. Hot and heady. Piping, smouldering hot. Do you know what I mean, Curtis?'

'Aye,' I said. 'Oh aye.'

He laughed bitterly.

'And then I married your mother, and all I had was cold meat and her mother's pickles.'

That night in my bedroom.

Blink and red beat of jet plane.

Splay of stars on skylight window.

And downstairs the voices.

On and on.

On and on and on.

Mother and mother's mother glaring at father.

Father deep in a book.

Smiling a contented smile.

Shaking his head with pleasure.

Mother's mother spoke.

'I blame you for Curtis, Vernon.'

'Sorry,' said father. 'You were saying?'

'It's no use, mother,' said my mother. 'He's reading a book.'

'He's never got his nose out of one,' said her mother. 'What's wrong with you, Vernon? What's wrong?'

'There's nothing wrong with me,' said my father chirpily.

'Oh yes there is,' said my mother.

'Oh no there isn't,' said my father.

'You see, you see,' said my mother's mother. 'Argue, argue, argue. All we get from him these days is defiance and argey bargey.'

Mother turned to father and pushed his shoulders hard.

'Our marriage is breaking up in front of you, Vernon, and all you can do is read books,' she said.

'I like reading books.'

'He's picked that up from Curtis,' said my mother's mother.

'I know,' said my mother. 'And that's not the only thing he's picked up from him.'

'Oh,' said the old bat. 'What else is there?'

'He's become argumentative. He's become dissatisfied. There are times, mother, when I can hardly tell him and Curtis apart.'

'Fancy.' said her mother.

'Look at those eyes. Just look at those eyes of his, mother. He seems to know something we don't.'

I hear things I didn't ought to hear.

The canal-side pub.

Shivering sunlight on the windy water.

Father and Sam sitting on the wall drinking their pints.

'Rivers, Sam. Rivers,' said father.

'What?'

'The Rhine! What a river, Sam. Eight hundred and twenty miles long. Navigable five hundred miles inland as far as Lake Constance. Its catchment area, including the delta, is more than 85,000 square miles. And that, Sam, is twice the size of Liberia.'

'What the hell are you on about, Vernon?'

'The Mekong,' said my father. 'There's another pearler of

a river. Two thousand five hundred miles long, Sam. Imagine it. Deep gushing mountain gorges. Paddy fields and water buffalo. Smokey-skinned women with smouldering almond eyes.'

'I don't follow you, Vernon.'

'They're from books, Sam,' said my father, his eyes gleaming. 'Rivers. Rivers to sail away from.'

'Away from where, Vernon?'

'Away from here,' said my father eagerly and intently. 'Me and Curtis. Sailing away from here on a great balsa raft, Sam. Bucking and bouncing over rapids. Fighting off caymen. Sparring with manatee. Struggling with . . .'

'Wait a minute, hold on, Vernon,' said Sam. 'What's Curtis got to do with all this?'

'He's my release, Sam,' said my father. 'He's my escape from here.'

I hear things I didn't ought to hear.

The back parlour.

Father and myself reading.

Mother and mother's mother glaring at us.

'He's evil,' said mother's mother.

'Oh, mother.'

'He is. He's evil. Wicked. He stares at you with those eyes of his, and it seems he's searching right into the cockles of your soul.'

Mother began to sob.

She sobbed uncontrollably.

'Oh mother,' she said. 'What a mess.'

Mrs Place sat down on the sofa and pointed at me.

'When I was little, Avril, we had a dog just like that,' she said. 'He used to sit himself in front of you and stare at you. Right into your eyes. Staring, staring, staring. Your grandfather couldn't stand it. He used to kick him up the bum with the toe of his boot. But he still did it. Staring,

staring, staring. We had to have him put down finally. We couldn't stand his staring.'

'But, mother. Curtis is not a dog. Curtis is human.'

'Human?' she said, her mother. 'Is he, Avril? Is he? Look what he's done to Vernon. Look at those eyes of his. Look, look.'

On the river bank once more.

Chiff chaff and black cap.

Moorhen and dabchick.

My father and myself.

'I stare into your eyes, and I can see things,' I said.

'What can you see, Curtis?' said my father softly yet fiercely.

'I can see anything you want me to see,' I said.

'Honest?'

'Honest.'

'Can you see what it was like the day I was born?'

'Oh yes,' I said. 'Squalls from the north east. Canal furrowed. Bleak gulls on bleak winter parks.'

The willow warbler burst into song.

A couple of days later my father and my mother were summoned once more to Mrs Mazarene's study.

Her pearl necklace glowed.

'I've asked you here to tell you that I feel Curtis's best interests would be served if for a while he were taken away from the environment of the family home,' she said.

'What?' said my father. 'Take Curtis away?'

'No, Mr Hemingway,' said Mrs Mazarene. 'It is not a case of taking Curtis away. It is a case of placing Curtis in an environment which allows his talents to express themselves to their fullest potential.'

My father leaned forward and beat his fist on the top of her desk.

'But his talents are expressed to their fullest potential,' he said. 'Look what he's done for me.'

'I beg your pardon, Mr Hemingway?' she said.

'Look at me,' he said. 'You see before you a new man. And it's Curtis what's done that. He's opened up new horizons for me with his books. The capital of Afghanistan – Kabul. The summer capital of Kashmir – Srinagar. Swallows and Amazons for ever, John and Susan, Roger and Kitty, Dick and Dorothea, Nancy and Peggy. Peggy? Poor Peggy. When I grow up, Mrs Mazarene, I intend to marry Peggy. I shall take her from her London bed-sit. I'll throw out all the empty bottles of gin. I'll rip off her dowdy tweeds. I'll dress her in silks and flimsy satin. I'll love her. I'll bury my head in her snow white thighs. I'll lick the plum red tips of her nipples. She'll be the Sunday roast of my life.'

The willow warbler sang in full flood.

Dragonflies hovered.

A mute swan hissed.

'You can't let them take you away from me, Curtis,' said my father.

'It's been arranged,' I said.

'But what'll happen to me? What about my future?'

'Take mine,' I said.

He opened his eyes wide.

'What?' he said.

'You can have my future. I don't want it.'

'I don't understand, Curtis,' he said.

'Clear off from here now,' I said. 'And take my future deep inside you.'

His eyes filled with tears.

He took hold of my hands and clasped them firmly.

'Do you really mean that, Curtis?' he said.

'Course I do, you daft berk,' I said. 'I've got such plans for you. You'll roam the world. You'll see its sights. You'll smell its smells – heady, hot and tangy. You'll make love to wild women – heady, hot and tangy.

'Take my future.

'You are a gifted man.'

They took him away on a Thursday morning.

It was raining.

The weeks passed.

I kissed Elisabeth at the back of the bike sheds.

I said I'd marry her, when she grew up, and we'd have a neat little house and everything would be just so.

One evening in the back parlour Mrs Place said to my mother:

'Don't fret about him, Avril.'

'I'm not, mother,' said my mother.

'Look at it this way, love. You've lost a husband, but you've gained a child.'

'I know,' said my mother.

'They'll look after him properly in the home he's been sent to.'

'I hope so,' said my mother.

'He'll have his own little room with his own little colour telly,' said Mrs Place. 'And they'll smile at him, if he starts his argey bargey. And they'll give him their shoulders to cry on, when he sobs and when he wails. You see, Avril, they've met hundreds of people like Vernon. They've got the medical knowledge and know-how to deal with a man who thinks he's a gifted adult.'

The phone rang.

I answered it.

It was my father.

'Hello, dad,' I said. 'Where are you ringing from?'

'Kabul,' he said, and then he put the receiver down.

'That was my dad,' I said.

'Oh yes,' said my mother. 'And where was he ringing from this time?'

'Kabul,' I said.

'Kabul?' said my mother. 'Where's Kabul?'

'Search me,' I said. 'I haven't the faintest idea.'

Chapter Twenty-five

That's what comes of marrying beneath your class.

Her husband's bunged in a home.

And then two months later her son's killed stone dead under the back wheels of a pantechnicon.

It's retribution, is that.

Am I right?

I am.

Still, it's no use crying over spilled milk.

She's getting over it quite well considering.

Hallam being here has done her all the good in the world.

There's been a great improvement.

Mind you, they were always close, were Hallam and Avril.

I always felt there was something more between them than brother and sister.

I loved him, Hallam.

I loved him more than Vernon.

I loved him from the day he was born.

I loved him from the moment he was brought home and I looked in his pram, and saw him staring at me, and there was laughter in his eyes, and he seemed to look at you as though he knew things we didn't know.

I used to take him out in his pram, and he never slept.

He was always wide awake, looking around him, taking notice, storing things up.

He never slept.

He always fought sleep.

He didn't cry when you put him to bed at nights. He just lay in his cot looking around him. If you crept upstairs so he couldn't hear and peered round the door into his bedroom, you'd see him wide awake, and there'd be a humorous and knowing smile on his face.

I loved him for that.

On the day I married Vernon, he stood in the church and when I walked down the aisle he looked at me and on his face was that humorous and knowing smile.

And I loved him for that.

I don't trust him.

He came round to our house a week ago and he told Garfield and me that he was going to take the whole family back to London with him for a treat.

A treat?

That sounds ominous.

Much to my surprise Garfield was delighted.

Usually he makes excuses for going out. Is he shy? Or does he hate people?

When we go on holiday, all he wants to do is to stick by me. He won't make friends. He won't talk to people. He leaves all that sort of thing to me. It's flattering in a way, I suppose.

But does he really want to be with me?

Or is he frightened of being on his own?

I've managed to arrange a short period of time off work at the shirt manufacturing factory.

I was quite surprised that Tarleton was agreeable, considering the shortness of the notice I gave him.

He said to me:

'Garfield, no problem, mate. Take three days. Take five days. No problem. Right?'

Why?

He's not going to replace me, is he?

They're not going to make me redundant?

Oh God, what if they make me redundant?

They won't make me redundant. They can't. My section's been second three times running. Maybe, they think we should have come first three times running. Is that why Tarleton didn't dance with Hazel at last year's dinner dance? He always used to. In fact, he always used to hold her too close for my liking. He used to hold her really close to him in the slow foxtrot and he'd look over her shoulder at me, and there'd be that grin on his face. I hated that grin. What if he fancied her? What if he expected me to . . . well, you know . . . to offer her to him. It's not all that outrageous. You hear of these things happening constantly in business. The boss expects his juniors to place their wives at his disposal. Droit de whatdoyoumacallit. Oh God, no. It's not that, is it?

Why does everyone fancy Hazel?

I know she's not like all the other wives. I think she despises them, if the truth be known. I don't know why she does. They seem a decent enough bunch to me.

Is that why she wears those low cut dresses when we go to the firm's functions?

Oh God, maybe that's what it is. Old man Roderick's noticed and he's told Tarleton and Tarleton's . . .

Why does everyone fancy Hazel?

I thought it was only Hallam who fancied Hazel.

I must be mad bringing them all to London.

I must be out of my mind.

Still, I owe them something, I suppose.

I haven't been a terribly efficient son/brother/brother-in-law.

I haven't been to all the funerals and weddings and christenings and crisis meetings and . . .

Here's a thought.

Have you noticed that a woman's tits are always the same colour as the back of her hands?

I wonder if that's true of Hazel.

Chapter Twenty-six

They had been in London for three days.

It was Mrs Place's birthday.

She was shopping in the West End with Hazel.

Hallam, Garfield and Avril remained in the flat, preparing a surprise for their mother.

In the drawing room Hallam Place pushed the Hoover with one hand. In the other hand he held a glass of whisky from which he drank deeply and appreciatively.

The sun was shining.

A canary sang in a distant room.

Garfield entered the drawing room from the bathroom. He was bare-footed. He carried a bowl of piping hot water.

He sat down in the maroon leather armchair, immersed his feet in the water and grunted with pleasure.

After a while Hallam said:

'What's the first thing she'll say?'

'Who?' said Garfield.

Hallam Place switched off the Hoover.

'Mother,' he said. 'What's the first thing she'll say when she walks through that door?'

'I haven't a clue.'

'Think.'

'I can't.'

Hallam Place pushed the Hoover away from him and took another long sip from his glass of whisky.

'All right,' he said. 'I'll tell you what she'll say. She'll come storming through that door, battle flags flying, all guns blazing and she'll say: "London! What a dump! Am I right? I am." That's what she'll say, Garfield. Right?'

Garfield shrugged his shoulders.

'I haven't a clue, mate,' he said.

Hallam Place glared at him.

His voice became fiercer and he slammed down his glass hard on the top of his work desk.

'She'll stand in the centre of the room, and the floodgates will burst open. All the prejudices. Too many Arabs in Marks and Spencers. Too many Germans treading on her heels in Oxford Street. Dirty carriages on the District Line. Unfriendly faces in the public toilets. I can just hear her. "And as for shopping in London. You go into a baker's, and they've got different names for all their breads. They don't know the meaning of barm cakes and pikelets. You go into a baker's shop down here, and he looks at you as though you're talking in a foreign language. Am I right? I am."'

He paused.

He looked to Garfield for some hint of approval or recognition, but his brother kept his eyes firmly fixed on his feet and grunted softly with contentment as the heat from the water seeped through the soles of his feet up through his ankles and soothed his calves.

Hallam Place poured himself another glass of whisky.

He spoke softly.

'On and on and on she'll go. No wonder she drove Vernon insane. "And they've got different programmes on the wireless down here. All you get on the wireless down here is Michael Aspel and the Nolan Sisters. The Nolan Sisters! They should be prosecuted. They should be . . ." Are you listening to me, Garfield?'

'Mm,' said Garfield.

'Listen, Garfield, for the first time in your life I'm giving you some home truths about our mother.'

'Leave off, Hallam.'

'You know what I'm trying to find? I'm trying to find that black box recorder buried deep inside her that'll reveal all, when we break it open and play over the tapes. Hey! That's a great idea, Garfield.'

'What?'

'We should all be born with a black box recorder implanted in the back of our brain like on an aeroplane. And during our lives it records every single thought, every action, every single deceit and dream, and when we die, they cut it out of our brain, open it up, play the tapes and, wop – THE TRUTH. Great idea, eh, Garfield?'

Garfield looked up from his bowl and said:

'What's got into you?'

'What's got into me?' said Hallam Place. 'I'll tell you what's got into me. I am examining my status. I am examining and questioning my life. I am questioning the lives of all those around me, little brother. I am questioning and challenging the lives of my nearest and dearest. Do you understand that, little brother?'

'Mm.' said Garfield.

'No, you don't,' screamed Hallam Place. 'You haven't the faintest idea of what I'm talking about. You're so cocooned in your bloody awful mediocrity, you haven't the remotest interest in anyone but yourself. You don't even know what your own mother will say when she walks through that door. I know what she'll say. She'll purse her lips and click her shoulders and she'll say: "What a day I've had. If there's one thing I detest, it's shopping in London. All those foreign tourists. Germans, Yanks, Darkies, Aussies. And they're all wearing those sticky-out rucksacks. I'd ban all rucksacks, if I had my way. And umbrellas. The number of times I've nearly had my eye poked out by . . ."'

'She won't say that,' said Garfield.

'What?'

'She won't say that. When mother walks through that door, the first thing she'll say is: "Garfield, what are you doing with your feet stuck in a bowl of hot water."'

'Yes, what are you doing?' snapped Hallam Place.

'Trying to get some relief,' said Garfield.

'I don't understand.'

'My feet are killing me. I've been tramping round London for three days solid. Shops, zoos, waxworks. Then more shops, more zoos, more waxworks. Sheer torture.'

'Thank you,' said Hallam Place.

'What do you mean?'

'Ye Gods, mate. I invite the whole lot of you to come and stay with me, and every one of you has done nothing but complain.'

At that moment Avril walked into the room from the kitchen.

'I can't do anything with this London water, you know.'

'You what?' shouted Hallam Place.

'This London water is so hard, I just can't get the grease off the pots.'

Garfield threw back his head and burst into laughter.

'And what's the matter with you?' said Avril coldly.

'It's him,' said Garfield, pointing to his brother. 'Old Mother Russia.'

'Old Mother Russia?' said Hallam Place. 'What the hell do you mean?'

'Well,' said Garfield. 'Ever since we've come down here, you've been fussing around us as though we're a load of peasants from deepest Siberia who've never seen running water or electricity in the whole of our lives. Well, Hallam, we are quite used to these amenities, you know. We do know how to work the immersion heater and the thermostat on the central heating.'

'I don't,' said Avril.

'What?' said Garfield.

'Well, it was so hot out there in the kitchen I started to

fiddle with the switch, and there was a terrible clicking noise and . . .'

'Oh my God,' said Hallam Place. 'Oh hell.'

And he dashed out to the kitchen.

I wish I hadn't come.

I feel so dowdy and dull.

Mother and Hazel are out shopping, and they look so neat and smart.

They wanted me to go with them.

How could I?

I hadn't the clothes for shopping in smart West End stores.

And, in any case, someone had to prepare the party.

It's mother's birthday today, you see, and we're giving her a surprise party.

Oh my God, that'll be a minefield.

Rows.

Argey, bargey.

'If only you'd married, Geoffrey Lancaster, we'd be having this party in the Ritz.'

On and on and on.

Hallam Place returned to the drawing room from the kitchen.

There was a broad smile on his face.

He walked straight to Avril and kissed her on the forehead.

'Thanks, Avril,' he said. 'It's absolutely smashing.'

'What is?' said Avril.

'The spread, you dum dum. It's terrific. Mother will be knocked out,' said Hallam Place, and he gave Avril a long, slow hug.

Avril smiled.

'I shouldn't bank on that,' she said. 'You know mother. "A party? Enjoyment? What's all this preoccupation with enjoyment? There's far too much enjoyment in the world these days."'

The brothers and their sister laughed.

'Let's have a drink,' said Hallam Place.

'Good idea,' said Garfield.

Hallam Place poured out three large whiskies and handed round the glasses.

'Well,' he said. 'How long is it since we've been all on our own like this?'

'God knows,' said Garfield.

'It's nice, isn't it?' said Avril.

'Tremendous,' said Garfield.

'Do you remember what we used to do when we were kids?' said Hallam Place.

'Yes,' said Avril. 'We'd play that game – "You Be Me And I'll Be You".'

'I was always Garfield,' said Hallam Place.

'And I was you,' said Avril.

'And I was lumbered with mother,' said Garfield.

They laughed with deep contentment.

'Let's drink a toast,' said Hallam Place. 'Brothers and sister – to us.'

They raised their glasses and were just about to drink the toast, when they heard the click of the key turning in the front door.

'Oh God, it's mother,' said Garfield, and they threw back their drinks in a single gulp.

They heard the two women entering the hall.

Hallam Place whispered to Garfield:

'Remember. What's the first thing she'll say when she walks through the door?'

The door burst open and in stepped Mrs Place.

She was followed by Hazel, heavily laden with parcels and boxes.

The first thing Mrs Place said was:

'Garfield. What are you doing with your feet stuck in a bowl of hot water?'

'Way hay, I won, I won.'

Mrs Place glowered at him.

'And what's wrong with you?' she said. 'Don't tell me. I don't want to know. Get your feet out of that bowl, put your socks on and help Hazel unpack your parcels.'

Garfield shrugged his shoulders and took his feet out of the bowl of water.

Mrs Place turned to Avril.

'By gum, Avril, I could just eat a nice Welsh rarebit,' she said. 'Have you got any Cheshire cheese in?'

'I don't know, mother,' said Avril. 'It's not my kitchen.'

'Typical. Absolutely typical,' said Mrs Place. 'I come home worn to a frazzle, my arms dropping off with lugging parcels, my feet like two lumps of raw steak, and there's neither sign nor light on the horizon of a decent Welsh rarebit.'

Hallam Place took his mother by the arm and led her to the sofa.

'Why don't you sit down and make yourself comfy, mother, and we'll rustle up something special for you.'

He winked at Avril, who repaired at once to the kitchen.

Mrs Place sat on the sofa and flicked her shoulders.

'I don't want anything special, Hallam,' she said. 'All I want is a decent Welsh rarebit with Yorkshire relish. I don't suppose you've got Yorkshire relish neither, have you? Typical. Absolutely typical.'

'Let me get you a drink, mother,' said Hallam Place.

'Not at this time of day,' said Mrs Place. 'Wait a minute. Have you been giving Avril drinks while I've been out?'

'She's just had a very small glass of whisky.'

'Typical. Absolutely typical,' said Mrs Place. 'Her first time in London for thirteen years, and you turn her into a raging alcoholic. I've read all about it in magazines, you know. These women who stay at home and drink cheap continental wine from Europe all day and get so blotto they can't . . .'

'She had one very small glass of whisky, for Christ's sake,' said Hallam Place.

'Don't you use language like that in front of me, young man,' said Mrs Place, and her eyes flashed with anger, and she flicked her shoulders. 'You might write comedy scripts for television, but you're still young enough to get a back-hander from me for using foul language. Am I right? I am.'

Hazel moved across and sat down next to Mrs Place.

She rested her hand on her shoulders.

'Come on, mum. Don't upset yourself,' she said. 'Tell the boys what sort of an afternoon we've had.'

'Horrendous. Absolutely horrendous,' said Mrs Place. 'London! What a dump! Am I right? I am.'

'You see, you see,' said Hallam Place triumphantly. 'What did I tell you?'

'Ah,' said Garfield. 'But mine came first.'

'What are you two talking about?' said Mrs Place. 'Don't tell me. I don't want to know. You're in cahoots, that's what you are. Am I right? I am.'

Hallam Place poured himself a drink with slow deliberation.

He took three slow sips from it.

Then he said:

'As a matter of fact, mother, you're right.'

'I beg your pardon?' said Mrs Place.

'Garfield and I are in cahoots because we've arranged a surprise for you.'

'A surprise?' said Mrs Place. 'What surprise? I don't like surprises. I'm well known for detesting surprises.'

'You'll like this one,' said Garfield.

'What is it?'

'A birthday party,' said Hallam Place.

'A birthday party?' said Mrs Place. 'Here? In a flat?'

'That's why I invited the whole tribe of you up here.'

'"Tribe?" Tribe – is that what you think of us?' said Mrs Place.

'For God's sake, mother,' said Hallam Place. 'I invited you here so you could have a marvellous and joyous and happy time on your birthday. It's your birthday today. I've arranged a party for you. Now bloody well enjoy it, for Christ's sake.'

What a family.

Honestly, I really did not know what I was letting myself in for, when I married Garfield.

Argey bargey, his mother calls it.

Well, that's all we had as we ate her birthday tea.

Why must families be so disputatious?

Why can't there be harmony?

There was in my family.

We were loving and kind and considerate to each other.

We hated rows.

We looked on rows as failures.

Not this family. Rows are meat and drink to them. Without rows they would fold up and disintegrate.

Mrs Place pushed away her plate and said:

'Well, that was without any exception the worst birthday tea I have ever had in my life.'

'Thank you very much indeed, mother,' said Avril. 'I spend all afternoon slaving away in the kitchen, and you turn round and throw that in my face.'

'I'm not talking about the food, Avril,' said Mrs Place. 'It was lovely. Really delicious. The sandwiches were a bit on the thick side, mind you, and I never have been that fond of greengages and custard, but all in all . . .'

'It was absolutely delicious, Avril,' said Hazel. 'You did us proud.'

Mrs Place sat back in her chair and narrowed her eyes.

'It's a pity some others I could mention didn't do us proud as well,' she said.

'Meaning what?' said Hallam Place.

Hazel laughed a bitter, icy little laugh.

'Meaning that you and Garfield completely spoiled your mother's birthday tea with all your stupid squabbling and arguing,' she said.

'Us?' said Hallam Place. 'Us?'

'Yes, you,' said Mrs Place. 'Hazel's quite right. I've never been so insulted in the whole of my life. And by my own sons, too. My own flesh and blood.'

'No one insulted you, mother,' said Garfield.

'Didn't they, Garfield? Didn't they?' said Mrs Place. 'Well, if you think calling your mother a typically, bigoted Northerner isn't . . .'

Hallam Place smacked the palm of his hand on the table.

'I did not call you a typically bigoted Northerner,' he said. 'I simply said I cannot stand the prejudice people like you show against anyone who steps a centimetre over the bounds of what you consider is normal.'

'Precisely, Hallam. Precisely,' said Mrs Place. 'But you didn't spend all afternoon battling against Arab shoplifters in British Home Stores, did you?'

Hallam Place sighed deeply.

'Shiftless, dirty lot, these Arabs,' continued his mother. 'They should be put up against a wall and shot. What are they doing living in our country in the first place, that's what I want to know? There's our boys from Canada and

Australia and New Zealand and South Africa who fought with us during the war against Musso the Wop, and they've got to have visas to live here. Yet you get these greasy, oily Gyppos coming over here with their cataracts and their fat, pock-marked wives and taking over the whole country. I'm not prejudiced. Far from it. I'm simply saying they should be put on a cattle boat and shipped off back to their own country.'

Hallam Place spread open the palms of his hands and said: 'I rest my case.'

'Don't be so bloody pompous,' said Hazel.

'Oh, leave him alone, Hazel,' said Mrs Place. 'There's no coping with him, when he's in one of these moods. It's living down south what's done it, you know.'

'I'm hearing things,' said Hallam Place. 'I must be.'

'No, you're not,' said Mrs Place. 'You've fallen under the influence of the Southerners hook, line and sinker. I never could abide the Southerners. Nesh lot, they are. Arrogant. Unfriendly. Rubbish at fish and chips.'

'Mother,' said Garfield. 'That is precisely what Hallam meant when he accused you of being prejudiced.'

'I am not being prejudiced,' said Mrs Place. 'And I don't want interruptions from you neither. Dear Lord above, he's only been in London three days, and he's acting like one of them already. Londoners! I can't abide them. They're the worst of the lot. I detest them.'

'I don't,' said Avril.

Mrs Place's mouth dropped open.

Hazel turned to her with astonishment on her face, Garfield coughed nervously, and Hallam Place smirked to himself.

'I beg your pardon, Avril?' said Mrs Place.

'I like Londoners,' said Avril firmly.

'Well, you would, wouldn't you?' said Mrs Place. 'Anything to be different. You married beneath you just so you could be different from everyone else. When I think of Geoffrey Lancaster, and what you could have done with your life, if you'd married him, it makes my blood boil. Literally.'

'Oh God, here we go again,' said Hallam Place.

'Never mind "here we go again",' said Mrs Place. 'If you'd had any regard for your sister here, you'd have put your foot down firmly when she said she was going to marry that funny little fellow with the big ears and no prospects. You'd have banned it. Sine die if necessary. You'd have backed me up, and sent him packing with a good kick up the flap – and that's swearing, is that.'

Avril jumped up from the table.

Her eyes were wide open, and she was breathing harshly.

She glared at her mother and wagged her finger in front of her nose.

'I like Londoners,' she shouted. 'I like them, I like them, I like them.'

They stared at her in shocked silence.

She banged the table.

'And I hate Geoffrey Lancaster,' she said. 'I hate him with fervour and with passion. And, if you go on talking like this, mother, I shall grow to hate you with fervour and with passion.'

And I will.

I shall grow to loathe her.

Look at her.

Will I have a mean mouth like that when I reach her age?

Will I have those creases of discontent at the corner of the mouth?

Will I have those restless eyes and those constantly drumming fingers?

Hallam got out.

That's what I wanted to do.

I married Vernon, but she wouldn't let me go.

He was a lovely man. He was a craftsman. He had craftsman's hands. And he was slow in bed like a craftsman.

He was full of love. There wasn't an ounce of hatred in him. He hated rows. He was gentle and considerate. He was so generous.

And she despised him.

Why did she loathe and hate him so much?

He wanted her love.

That's the only thing he wanted. He couldn't understand why she would never give him a chance to show it.

Every move he made however timid she snarled at him and snapped at him.

That's what destroyed him.

She would never take his love.

Chapter Twenty-seven

The women cleared the table and washed the pots in silence.

The men stayed in the drawing room and drank wine in silence.

Dusk sidled in from the common with the soft hoots of tawny owl and the scream of swifts.

The women came in from the kitchen and were offered wine by Hallam Place.

Mrs Place refused with a sniff and a flick of her shoulders.

Hazel took her glass with a smile. So did Avril.

There was a knock on the front door.

'Good,' said Hallam Place. 'They're here.'

'Are you expecting visitors?' said Hazel.

'That's right,' said Hallam Place.

'On your mother's birthday?' said Mrs Place.

'Yes,' said Hallam Place. 'They've come to the party.'

'But I thought you said this was a family party,' said Mrs Place. 'Why do you want strangers coming to a family party? Don't tell me. I know what it is. Your own family aren't good enough for you, are they? You've got to have outsiders in before you can enjoy it, is that what it is? I suppose they'll be southerners, too. Either that or they'll be Arabs, and they'll pinch all your apostle tea spoons.'

There was another knock at the front door.

It was more urgent this time.

'They have come specially to see you, mother,' said Hallam Place.

'Me?' said Mrs Place. 'But they're strangers. I don't know them. I'm well known for not knowing strangers.'

Hallam Place smiled.

'They're my surprise for you, mother,' he said. 'They are my birthday present. Now sit tight, prepare yourself for an evening's enjoyment, and I'll let them in.'

He smiled once more and left the drawing room for the hall.

Mrs Place looked from face to face and the corners of her mouth creased, and she sniffed.

'Enjoyment!' she said scornfully. 'What's all this preoccupation with enjoyment? There's far too much enjoyment in the world these days. That's what's wrong with it. That's where so many of the world's ills come from. If people weren't so relentlessly pursuing enjoyment at the expense of everything else in life, you'd still be able to buy decent potted shrimps and you'd still get Big Bill Campbell and His Rocky Mountain Rhythm on the wireless and . . . Present? What does he mean, Hazel?'

'Ah, that's Hallam, mum,' said Hazel. 'Has anyone ever known what he means?'

I haven't.

I'm his brother, and I've never really understood.

We used to play this game You Be Me And I'll Be You, and he played all our parts perfectly.

He played them better than us.

It was as though he was us.

He was mother with her nidgety voice and her sniff and her twitching shoulders.

He was Avril with her resentful shoulders and the half-choked smile in her voice.

He was me with my stuttering and my mumbling and my apologetic thumbs.

He was everyone without any problem.

But, of course, Garfield.

Of course, I was.

That's the whole point of the proceedings.
So now, my dear family, meet the strangers.
Meet yourselves.

Chapter Twenty-eight

Silence.

Darkness save for the soft glow of the standard lamp in the corner of the drawing room by the upright book shelves.

Okay, Hazel, here's your chance.

The writer of comedy scripts gives you the chance to change your story.

See if you are a stranger to yourself.

I'd live with him here in Wimbledon.

Early every evening he would undress me.

We would go to bed, and we would make love all night.

He'd be gentle, and he'd be fierce.

We'd invent things.

I would be a slinky Oriental lady with dark, smouldering almond eyes.

I would be a courtesan with rouged cheeks and a big black beauty spot.

I would be a tart.

And what would he be?

He'd just be Hallam, the literary lion, the man of the letters, the Bohemian in a centrally-heated garret, the sneerer, the cynic, the outsider, the manipulator of dreams.

He would laugh at my conceits.

He would serve my body, and I would writhe and contort, and I would arch my back, and I would cry out.

During the day, I would leave him alone whilst he wrote.

I'd bring him a mug of coffee from time to time, and at lunch I'd bring him in a glass of chilled hock, and we'd talk about his work.

We'd buy a Newfoundland dog, and I'd take him long, solitary walks on the common and watch him swim in the cool, black lakes and roll on his back in the cool, rabbit-cropped glades.

What sort of food would he eat?

I don't know his tastes.

They won't be like Garfield's, that's for sure.

'Oh no, Hazel. Keep it simple. You know how green peppers bring on my burps.'

Bastard, Garfield.

Bastard, bastard, bastard.

The school dance twenty-five years ago.

Why didn't he take me home when he had the chance?

Was he frightened of me? Did he dislike me? Did he fancy someone else that night?

Did he never fancy me?

Oh yes.

I fancied you something chronic that night, Hazel.

I fancy you now.

Show me how to take your bra off.

Let me look while you take off your clothes.

Lovely lady.

Lovely wife to my lovely brother.

Garfield?

What about you, mate?

Here's your chance.

I'd like to be single and live with my brother here in his flat at Wimbledon.

I certainly wouldn't be in shirts.

I think what I would like is to be in classified ads on a newspaper. That's what Greenwood does on *The Evening Telegraph and Argus*. He tells me it can be very interesting at times. You get a firm's car, and you travel extensively in the newspaper's circulation area.

I should like to travel extensively in the firm's car.

Of course, there would be the problem of garaging here and hereabouts. Most people seem to park their cars in the street. Lock-up garages, they tell me, are at a premium. Still, if I got good under-sealing I don't suppose much harm would come to the car.

I think he'd rather like me living here with him. I wouldn't get in his way, of course. If he had some of his famous writing or acting friends round to dinner or for after-pub drinks, I should keep well out of the way.

Well, I don't like meeting people.

Socially, I mean.

I quite like meeting people professionally.

But that's rather different, isn't it?

So, if he had people round, I'd go to my room and listen to the radio.

I'd be useful, too, if we got a dog.

You see, when he had to be away at nights on location filming and rehearsals and things like that, I'd be here to look after the dog, and he'd save a fortune on kennelling.

I'd like a Rhodesian Ridgeback.

Don't ask me why.

I don't know much about them except that they're supposed to hunt lions in their country of origin.

I suppose now they'll call them Zimbabwean Ridgebacks.

Hey, that's not a bad joke, is it?

I don't normally tell jokes.

I certainly wouldn't tell jokes if I lived here with Hallam. Well, he's the humorist in the family, isn't he?

He's the joker.

*   *   *

The joker in the pack?

Nice one, Garfield.

The one who got away, old man Garlick said, didn't he?

Avril tried to get away.

She failed.

Well, here you are, love.

Have another go.

I'd marry Geoffrey Lancaster.

There, that surprises you, doesn't it?

Well, that is what I would do.

I'd marry him in the cathedral with full choir and a fleet of Rolls-Royce and Daimlers.

We'd have a reception at the Gulliford Grange Country Club followed by a honeymoon in Barbados.

The full works, my loves.

And what a house we'd have.

An old sandstone mansion tastefully converted to gracious modern living including eight bedrooms (one master with bathroom en suite) drawing room, living room, kitchen with Aga, large utility room, walled garden and a range of interesting outbuildings and garaging for three cars.

I'd have my own car, of course.

And I'd supervise the garden.

I'd like that.

I'd make a rose garden. Not a rose garden full of rows and rows and rows of neat suburban roses.

No, it would be full of the old roses – damask roses, provence roses, moss roses, bourbon roses and tiny china roses.

It would smell superb.

And as for children?

Well, yes, I suppose we'd have children.

Dull, smug children. Middle of the road children. No trouble children. Good as gold children.

And we would all live a happy and a contented and a successful life, and everyone would say how suited we were.

And, of course, I would have my lovers.

And I would bring them here to this flat in Wimbledon and we would screw shamelessly.

What wild rampant lovers I would have – Dyson, Greenhough, Parkin, Statham, Tattersall, Tyldesley and, of course, J. A. Fallows.

And I'd be shameless with them.

I'd lick them in parts other tongues had never reached.

Oh, what my finger tips would do for them.

Boy oh boy.

And I'd be shameless, too, and reckless in all manner of other things.

I'd ring them up at work. I'd leave messages on their answering machines. I'd ring them up at home. I'd talk to their wives and their children and their au pairs and their baby sitters.

I'd sit outside their houses in my car.

I'd follow them in my car when they went out on their family outings.

And then, when their smug, dull, middle of the road, no trouble, good as gold marriages were destroyed, I'd laugh.

Wow, how I'd laugh.

And I'd still be laughing when I walked out on Geoffrey Lancaster and set up my stall here in this flat with my brother, Hallam.

And you, mother?

What plans would you make?

In your hands to change us all.

In your hands to give us happy endings or sad endings.

Yours to choose our fate.

I give you the power.

What will you do with it?

Nothing, of course.
I love you just the way you are.
You'll all do for me.
Am I right?
I am.

Chapter Twenty-nine

Next day we went home.

Oh, I did enjoy the party.

I must say those strangers Hallam invited round made all the difference.

They were just like us.

Wasn't it thoughtful of him?

He's a good lad when you get down to brass tacks.

They're all good in their own ways.

And it was so nice being all together like that on my birthday.

It was really conducive.

Am I right?

I am.

We went by mini-cab to the station, and then we caught the High Speed Train.

And do you know what?

I got talking to this very interesting lady.

Apparently she was going to the wedding of the daughter she'd not seen since the father walked out with her when he discovered she'd been having affairs right, left and centre with all and sundry in the neighbourhood and . . .

Never mind.

I'll tell you about it some other time.

THE WORLD'S GREATEST NOVELISTS NOW AVAILABLE IN GRANADA PAPERBACKS

Angus Wilson

The Strange Ride of Rudyard Kipling (non-fiction)	£1.95	☐
Hemlock and After	£1.50	☐
No Laughing Matter	£1.95	☐
The Old Men at the Zoo	£1.95	☐
The Middle Age of Mrs Eliot	£1.95	☐
Such Darling Dodos	£1.50	☐
Setting the World on Fire	£1.95	☐

J B Priestley

Angel Pavement	£2.50	☐
Bright Day	£2.25	☐
Saturn Over The Water	£1.95	☐
Lost Empires	£1.95	☐
It's an Old Country	£1.95	☐
The Shapes of Sleep	£1.75	☐
The Good Companions	£2.50	☐

John Barth

The Sot-Weed Factor	£1.95	☐
Giles Goat-Boy	£2.95	☐
The End of the Road	£1.50	☐
The Floating Opera	£1.95	☐
Letters	£3.95	☐